TEDDY BEA

Harrison Phillips is an English author of extreme horror and splatterpunk fiction. His literary influences range from Clive Barker and Stephen King, to Jack Ketchum and Edward Lee. He was born and raised in Birmingham, England, where he still resides with his long-suffering wife, their two daughters, and a schnauzer named Minnie.

www.twitter.com/harrisonhorror

www.facebook.com/harrisonphillipshorror

vestigialpress@hotmail.com

Copyright © 2022 Vestigial Press

Cover artwork by
InsaneCamel
(insanecamelcorp@gmail.com)

Harrison Phillips has asserted his right to be identified as the author of this work.

All rights reserved. This book, or any portion thereof, may not be reproduced or used in any manner, without the express written permission of the publisher.

This book is a work of fiction. All names and characters are the product of the authors imagination. Any resemblance to actual persons, living or dead, is entirely coincidental.

TEDDY BEARS PICNIC

If you go down to the woods today,
You better not go alone,

It's lovely down in the woods today,
But safer to stay at home,

For every bear there ever was,

Will gather there for certain because,

Today's the day the teddy bears
Have their picnic.

PROLOGUE

Melissa ran.

Naked, she ran as fast as her legs could carry her. Pain surged through her body. Blood oozed from the deep gash in her shoulder, where the blade had scraped against the scapula, separating skin from bone. As she ran, the dirt of the forest floor - mostly broken tree branches, sharp where the wood had splintered and snapped - dug into the soles of her bare feet. Occasionally, one of those broken tree branches would spring up under her weight and collide painfully with her calf or the bone of her shin.

But that was nothing. It was fine. She could take the pain. She *had* to. If she didn't, she might end up dead, just like Eddie.

How could this have happened? What had they done to deserve this?

It was the middle of July. For the entire day the sun had blazed overhead. Melissa and Eddie had been camping in the forest. Eddie had pitched their tent that very morning, in a small clearing they'd found. He'd built a campfire, over which they'd cooked spaghetti from a can. Once they had eaten, they had climbed to the nearest peak, where Melissa had spread out a blanket so that they could lie back and watch as the universe expanded before their eyes, while they waited for the sun to set. From their vantage point, they had had a full view of the thick forest that surrounded them. They had been drinking fruit cider. Eddie had brought a small bag of weed with him, so they'd smoked a couple joints. As the sun had set beyond the horizon, the cloudless sky turned from blue to orange, then to the most spectacular shade of purple. And then they had laid there, counting the stars above them.

Melissa was from the city. She hated it there; too much noise, too many people. At night, in the city, you could barely even *see* the stars. In the city, the bright haze of the streetlights and neon shop signs seemed to form a dense fog, which hung lazily above the rooftops, blocking out all but the brightest of stars. Melissa hoped that one day she might escape the city, to move to somewhere more rural. She hoped Eddie would come with her. But there was plenty of time for that; she was only nineteen after all.

It was so quiet and peaceful. If you listened close enough, you could just about hear the animals moving between the trees – deer and badgers, no doubt - blissfully unaware of the humans sitting just a few feet away.

As Melissa had laid there, listening to the silence and enjoying the fresh, clean air that filled her lungs, Eddie had positioned himself above her, propped up on his elbow. He lowered himself down and kissed her.

Melissa wrapped her arms around Eddie's neck and pulled him in tight, kissing him deeply, her tongue slipping into his mouth.

Eddie slid his hand under her dress. She'd been wearing a woollen, black-and-white striped jumper dress, which stopped mid-thigh. She'd paired this with black knee-high socks. She thought she looked cute. As Eddie's fingertips brushed lightly against her stomach, the bite of the cool air raised goosebumps on her skin, a light breeze fluttering beneath her clothes. She'd chosen not to wear a bra, and now her nipples were hard. Eddie pinched them gently, as he caressed the flesh of her breasts.

Melissa pulled her face away. "Is it just me?" she said. "Or is it getting cold?"

"I don't know," said Eddie, his hand slipping downwards over Melissa's stomach, then sliding under the elastic of her panties. "Is it?"

Melissa bit her lip and nodded. She took a sharp breath as Eddie's fingers entered her.

"Yeah," said Eddie, answering his own question. "Maybe you're right. You think we should head back?"

Melissa nodded once again.

Eddie smiled. He pulled his hand from out of her pants. "Okay," he said, before kissing her deeply once again. "Let's go."

Eddie stood. He helped Melissa to her feet, before gathering up the blanket. They then scooted, hand in hand, back down the hill, to the clearing where they had made camp.

Melissa was giggling like a schoolgirl as she scrambled into the tent. Eddie quickly crawled in behind her, not bothering to zip the opening. And then they were on their hands and knees, kissing once again, pulling at each other's clothes.

Melissa pulled Eddie's t-shirt up over his head and tossed it aside. She then lifted off her own dress. Eddie was upon her then, pushing her back, flat onto the ground. He squeezed her breasts, rolling her nipples between his fingers, as he kissed and nuzzled at her neck. He then shifted downwards, kissing every inch of her body. Kneeling between her legs, he slid his hands under her buttocks, hooked his fingers under the waistband of her pants and pulled them off.

Melissa tipped her head back and gasped, as Eddie began to lap at her vagina, his tongue encircling her clitoris, probing her. Melissa ran her fingers through Eddie's scruffy hair, pulling him in towards her pelvis.

After a few minutes of intense pleasure, Melissa sat up and pulled Eddie's head from between her legs. She then dragged him down on top of herself. "So," she said, kissing him between almost every word. "Are you gonna fuck me, or what?"

"Oh, you bet I am," said Eddie, as Melissa pulled open his jeans and reached into his boxer shorts. His penis was already erect. "However…"

Melissa pushed Eddie away. "However? However… What?"

"However… I've gotta go take a piss."

"Seriously?"

"Seriously. I'll be, like, two minutes."

Melissa sighed. "You best be," she said, the disappointment audible in her voice.

"I will be." Eddie turned and pushed his way back out of the tent. "Jesus, it's cold out here now. Pass me my t-shirt."

Teddy Bears Picnic

"I don't think I should," said Melissa, a smirk etched to her face. "Maybe I should let you get cold, then you'll *have* to hurry back."

"I won't come back at all if I freeze to death."

Melissa smiled. She balled up Eddie's t-shirt and threw it at him. He then pulled it over his head and stood. "I'll be two minutes," he said, as he headed for the trees.

"Do you think you could *fuck me* for a bit longer than two minutes this time?" called Melissa, the sarcasm layered thick.

"Probably not," shouted Eddie. Then he was gone, his footsteps trailed off into nothing.

Melissa puffed out her cheeks and sighed. She laid flat on her back and pulled off her socks, rolling them down past her knees before doing so. She reached into her bag and retrieved her mobile phone. No network. She hadn't had signal since they'd entered the woods. Sighing once again, Melissa set her phone aside and closed her eyes.

Outside, the trees rustled and rattled as the night's breeze swept through the woods. Somewhere in the distance, an owl hooted.

And then there was another sound.

Footsteps.

Melissa smiled to herself. She couldn't wait for Eddie to get back. She couldn't wait to feel him inside her. "Hey! Get in here!" she said. "I'm cold. I need you to come warm me up."

Nothing. Eddie didn't reply.

"Eddie? What are you doing?"

Still nothing.

Melissa sat up. She turned her body around and sat up onto her knees. "Eddie? What's going on?"

He was standing outside the opening, motionless, little more than a silhouette.

Melissa crept forwards, scooting her palms across the groundsheet. "Eddie?"

Suddenly, the loose folds of material whipped open and something heavy landed in Melissa's lap, splattering a warm, wet liquid across her breasts.

Melissa screamed.

Eddie's severed head lay in her lap, his glassy, lifeless eyes staring up at her. His neck had been hacked open, his skin ragged and roughly torn. Part of his vertebrae protruded from the wound. His blood - now smeared across her chest - pooled in the valley formed by her thighs.

The shape outside the tent moved. Not Eddie. Somebody else. Some*thing* else. Footsteps crunched through the dirt of the forest floor, encircling the tent.

Melissa's heart began to race, thundering painfully in her chest. She scrambled onto her hands and knees, leaving Eddie's head to roll to the floor, to splash in the puddle of blood that had formed on the groundsheet. *What the fuck is going on?* thought Melissa. *Who's out there? Why are they doing this? What do they want?*

A shadow moved around the outside of the tent. Melissa scooted around, keeping her eyes on it at all times. She *needed* to get out of there somehow. She *needed* to escape the tent and run.

But then the shadow loomed taller over the tent, as if the person casting it were growing in size. With a deafening *rip*, the fragile material of the tent was torn in two. The first thought Melissa had was that this was some kind of animal, its razor-sharp claws tearing through the fabric with ease. But then there was a flash of light; moonlight reflected from steel.

A knife.

Melissa rolled to her front and tried to push with her legs, but a weight landed upon her. She felt the blade of the knife tear through the flesh of her left shoulder. She felt it scrape against the bone beneath.

Melissa screamed once again.

With all her might, adrenaline surging through her body, she forced herself up. She pushed herself out of the tent and onto her feet.

Then she ran.

With a quick glance over her shoulder, she saw the man emerge from the remains of the now collapsed tent. *Was that a man?* It was hard to tell through the darkness. It was certainly man-shaped, but the silhouette it cut seemed rough and undefined. But it was a knife that had sliced through her flesh, not the claws of some savage beast, of that she was sure.

Melissa ran as fast as the muscles in her legs would allow. The rough terrain of the forest floor dug into the soles of her feet. She could feel the blood pumping out of the wound in her shoulder, pouring down her back and between her buttocks.

She had no clue as to where she was going. It didn't matter; she just needed to get away.

She glanced over her shoulder. The man - the *thing* - was still behind her. Melissa took a deep breath. She clenched her teeth and pushed on.

CRUNCH!

It was as if the ground gave way beneath her. Her foot dropped awkwardly into a hole, half way up her calf. As her foot hit the bottom of the hole, her ankle turned over. A loud crack indicated that she had broken at least one bone. A searing pain burned through her leg.

She hit the ground hard, her face slamming painfully into the dirt. She tried to scream, but no sound came. She rolled over and pushed back, dragging her lame leg out of the hole. She pushed with every remaining ounce of strength she had.

But it was too late.

The man... The monster... Whatever it was, it was already upon her.

It was too dark to see anything meaningful, even this close up. As the beast bared down on her, she grabbed at its soft, shapeless form. Her fingers slid through what felt like animal fur. *What kind of animal can wield a knife?*

Melissa raised her hands, an attempt to protect herself. But she was too exhausted to fight. The blade of the knife penetrated the side of her neck.

At that moment, Melissa could no longer breathe. Everything went dark. She became light-headed, her brain fuzzy, as if all the blood had been drained from it.

And perhaps it *had*. Melissa could feel the warmth of her blood as it oozed from the gash in her neck and cascaded down her chest, her breasts and stomach slick with crimson. She couldn't move; she was as good as dead. All she could do was stare up at the *thing* that towered over her. She could only stare into those beady black eyes.

And then a sudden rush of agony as the blade was torn forwards, shredding through her larynx.

And then nothing.

Just death.

ONE

Abbie woke to the sound of her alarm beeping, her phone buzzing noisily on the wooden floor beside her. Groaning, she rolled over so that her left arm draped out of the bed, and, without even looking, she flicked her finger across the screen to silence the alarm. It was the same every morning; she always placed her phone in the exact same position, so she could get to the alarm as quickly as possible. She could probably turn it off now, even if she'd woken to find herself blind.

For a moment she considered the possibility of falling back to sleep. She felt as though she'd been dreaming. Of what, for the life of her she couldn't remember. It had been a nice dream though; of that she was certain. And the extra sleep would do her good; it was exactly what she needed right now.

But she couldn't. She'd set her alarm for 6:30, and Bex was due to pick her up at 8:00. She *had* to get up.

With another groan, her eyes still firmly shut, Abbie flipped the duvet off of herself, swung her legs out of the bed and stood.

Stretching, she slowly opened her eyes and looked at herself in the full-length mirror that hung on the back of the cupboard door. Standing there in her pyjamas - her hair tousled from sleep, her skin pale - she thought she looked tired. But she didn't need to see herself to know that; she could *feel* the exhaustion in her bones. Perhaps, she thought, she was also looking old. She was only twenty-three, but, sometimes, she felt more like she was eighty-three.

She needed a shower, that was all.

She pulled off her pyjamas and dropped them onto the pile of clothes that had accumulated in the corner of the room. That was the washing pile; she told herself she would take care of it once she got back from the trip.

She showered and washed her hair. Feeling refreshed, a towel wrapped tightly around her body, she sat on the edge of the bed and blow-dried her hair, once again looking at herself in the mirror. She looked better, she told herself. She looked refreshed. Perhaps that was the best she could hope for.

Things had been hard these past couple of months. She should've been glad that Will had gone; *he* had cheated on *her*, she had to remind herself. But she couldn't help but miss him. She missed waking up beside him, wrapped up in his arms. She missed those occasions when they showered together. She missed having him there to tell her that she looked good, not having to tell herself that (and feeling as if she was only lying to herself).

But that skank bitch had stolen him from her. She'd fucking well ruined her life.

Bex had arranged a little getaway for them, along with a handful of their closest friends. The idea, according to Bex, was to help her 'get over it'. Abbie wasn't entirely convinced that it was going to help. Still, a change of scenery wouldn't do any harm.

Abbie tied her hair up into a bun then dressed herself in denim shorts and a black, loose-fitting t-shirt. The sun was shining outside and the forecast said it was to remain this way for the entirety of the weekend.

She then packed a rucksack, folding her clothes and placing them in as neatly as possible. She packed a small bag of cosmetics, as well as her toothbrush and a can of deodorant. She didn't need anything else; Bex had said she'd take care of everything.

Abbie picked up her rucksack, flung it onto her back and headed downstairs. In the kitchen, she dropped her bag onto the floor, retrieved a glass from the drying rack and poured herself a glass of orange juice. That would be all she'd have for breakfast. If her mother had seen, she'd have been mortified; she'd have probably tried to force a full English down her throat, scared to death that her only daughter might waste away to nothing. Abbie sipped her juice, thinking about the fact that she'd soon have to leave this place; she and Will had signed the lease together, but now she could hardly afford the rent by herself. She might even have to move back in with her overbearing mother, God forbid. She finished the juice and placed the glass into the sink.

The doorbell rang. Abbie turned and looked down the hallway, to where she could see the front door. A silhouette passed before the glass; Bex, no doubt.

Abbie headed for the front door, released the latch and opened it up.

Sure enough, Bex stood before her.

Bex was really pretty. She was tall and skinny, and she had short black hair, cut into a bob. She was wearing skinny jeans and a crop top. "Hey!" she said, smiling excitedly. "What's up? You ready?"

Abbie nodded. "Uh huh. Let me just grab my bag." Quite why she hadn't brought it from the kitchen with her, she didn't know. She turned and headed back along the hallway.

"Okay," Bex called from the front door. "Do you need my help with anything?"

"Erm… No. I got it, thanks."

Abbie picked up her bag, slung it over one shoulder and returned to the front door. As she approached, Bex looked her up and down. "Is that it?" asked Bex. "Are you travelling light or somethin'?"

"No," said Abbie, dropping the rucksack from her shoulder and holding it in front of herself. "I've got everything I need."

"Seriously?" said Bex, her eyebrows raised. "Wow. Okay. I think I'd need about eight of those bags to fit all *my* stuff in."

"You're kidding, right?" asked Abbie, fairly certain that she was. But with Bex, anything was possible. She had always been spontaneous and tended to do things on the slightest of whims. It wouldn't be entirely surprising if she *had* brought enough stuff to fill eight bags.

"Hmmm… Maybe that is a *slight* exaggeration."

"*Very* slight, yeah?"

"*Very!*"

The two girls burst out laughing. Bex was funny. She was clever too. Smart, funny and extremely pretty - Abbie often wished she was more like Bex.

"Come on," said Bex. "Joe and Mike are waiting in the car."

"Mike?" said Abbie. "I thought you said Mike wasn't coming." Abbie had a sneaky suspicion that Bex was hoping to set her up with Mike. Truthfully, she had been glad when Bex had informed her that he could no longer make it. Not that Abbie was totally against getting into another relationship - and Mike was a decent enough guy - but she just wasn't ready.

"Change of plans. I'm not exactly sure what happened, but I think that once Joe told him that *you* were coming, he suddenly decided he *could* make it after all."

"Great." Abbie stepped out of the house. She closed the front door behind her and locked it. "And what about Gemma and Scott?"

"They're still meeting us there."

"Okay. Let's not keep them waiting then."

Bex chuckled. "Are you joking? This is Gemma we're talking about. I guarantee we'll beat them there. And I guarantee it'll be *them* keeping *us* waiting."

***

Joe's car was almost brand new. He'd only owned it for a few months, and it was less than a year old when he'd bought it. Bex hadn't been happy about it. She and Joe had been together for years now. She'd hoped that they might buy a house together soon, instead of renting. But, while she had been saving hard to build up their deposit, Joe had decided he was going to buy himself a nice, new car on finance. And he'd been complaining ever since they'd hit the country roads - those that had been well-used and poorly maintained, littered with potholes. It was understandable really; Abbie wouldn't want to drive her car on a road like this either, and it was nowhere near as new as his. But Joe made sure to let his feelings be known, with statements such as *'I bet my fuckin' exhaust is hanging off now'* and *'this best not fuck up my suspension'* and *'I'm gonna need new tyres after this'*.

"Just ignore him," Bex told Abbie. "I think he loves this car more than me."

Abbie didn't speak much during the journey. For the most part, she spent the time staring out of the window, watching the dense forest flashing by. Occasionally, the car would jerk as it hit a bump in the road, breaking her from her thoughts and causing Joe to utter something along the lines of *'for fuck's sake!'*.

Mike was sitting in the passenger seat, while Abbie and Bex were in the back. Mike had tried to initiate a conversation with Abbie on a handful of occasions. She felt bad, but she wasn't really in the mood for idle chit-chat. She replied politely, but did her best to cut those conversations as short as possible.

They pulled into the car park a little over two-and-a-half hours after having set off. The car park itself wasn't anything to get excited about, just an open space set back amongst the trees, a few meters off the road. The tyres of the car crunched through the dirt as Joe parked up on one side of the clearing. He made sure to position the car *between* the trees. "Hopefully," he said, as he applied the handbrake. "The birds won't shit all over my car here."

Abbie climbed out of the vehicle. She wasn't sure if it was the fresh air, or just the fact that she'd been sitting down for the better part of three hours, but she felt exhausted all of a sudden. She stretched her arms out wide and yawned.

Bex, Joe and Mike exited the car too. No sooner had his feet hit the ground, then Joe groaned, stretching his arms up high and twisting his torso from side to side. "Shit," he said. "My back is killin' me."

Bex wrapped her arms around Joe's waist and pulled herself in tight. "Maybe I'll give you a massage later," she said, a cheeky grin on her face. "If you're lucky."

"I'll look forward to it," said Joe, before kissing Bex firmly on the lips.

"Oh, God," said Abbie, rolling her eyes. "Get a room, you two."

"Yeah," agreed Mike. "I really hope we don't have to listen to you two having sex all weekend."

Joe pulled himself away from Bex, bursting into a fit of laughter. "You might have to, yeah!"

"No," said Bex. "They definitely *won't* be listening to that."

"They might."

Bex jabbed her elbow into Joe's ribs. "They won't. Trust me."

Laughing, Abbie and Bex made their way to the back of the car. Joe and Mike followed. There, Joe popped open the boot, then he and Mike began unloading the bags, dealing them out to their respective owners. Abbie took her rucksack and slung it onto her back. Bex had a rucksack and a holdall. "Is that everything?" asked Bex, as she hoisted the rucksack onto her shoulders.

"Looks like it," said Joe. "But if it just so happens that you *have* forgotten anything, well, you'll just have to do without. Hey, did you remember to pack your hairdryer?"

Bex offered a wide, sarcastic grin. "Ha ha," she said, her lack of amusement painfully obvious. "You're *hilarious*."

"Don't I just know it!"

Bex poked out her tongue.

"Anyway," said Abbie, changing the subject. "Do we know where Gemma and Scott are?"

"Nope," said Mike. "No idea."

"Well, they're late."

"Yeah, so I see. But it's not as if we can go on without them - Scott's supposed to be our 'fearless leader'. I wouldn't even know which direction we should start walking."

Bex pulled her phone from her back pocket. "I'll give Gem a call, see where they're at."

"You'll be lucky to get a signal out here," said Mike, ever the pessimist.

"I've got full signal, actually."

"Well, I guarantee that you won't in there." He pointed into the dense forest that surrounded them.

"Well then," said Bex, as she scrolled through the list of contacts on her phone, stopping when she reached Gemma's number. She pressed 'dial' and held the phone to her ear. "We best hope we don't get lost then, huh?"

TWO

Gemma sat in the passenger seat, with her feet up on the dash, the cool air rushing in through the open window, ruffling her skirt around her thighs. Her long, blonde hair whipped across her face, forcing her to brush it back behind her ears every few seconds. As annoying as this was, the sun was still blazing overhead, so the breeze was entirely welcomed.

Scott was in the driver's seat beside her, his attention entirely focused on the road ahead. It was understandable really - the road on which they were currently driving was barely wide enough for one car, let alone two. Gemma herself hated driving on country lanes such as this, so had been wholly grateful when Scott had volunteered to drive. Not that he'd have ever *expected* her to drive; he was Gemma's personal chauffeur, of course.

Gemma adjusted the sunglasses perched upon her nose; a bead of sweat had caused them to slip to an uncomfortable position halfway down the bridge. She flipped the page of her magazine, the wind causing the paper to rattle noisily until it was finally settled against the preceding page. She read her horoscope; she was born in October, so she was a Libra. "Hey, listen to this," she said, drawing Scott's attention briefly from the road.

"What?" said Scott, somewhat annoyed that she had broken his concentration.

"According to this " said Gemma, a sly smirk creeping on her face. "I'm going to hook up with the man of my dreams this weekend." She loved teasing Scott like this. She knew *he* didn't believe in astrology *at all* - Gemma was only *half-serious* about it herself - but she knew he'd always take this sort of bait. All she had to do was reel him in.

"Is that right?" Scott rolled his eyes, despite the fact that Gemma wouldn't see this behind his own sunglasses. He itched the stubble that lined his chin.

"Apparently so." Gemma spoke matter-of-factly, as if whatever the horoscope said would happen was entirely inevitable. "According to this, Venus and the Sun are in perfect alignment, so, basically, it's one-hundred percent guaranteed to happen."

"Yeah? Well, if me and you have sex this weekend, then I guess your horoscope *will* have come true, since I *am* the man of your dreams, right?"

"Well, I mean - *yeah*. Of course. But, this kind of implies that it'll be somebody I've only just met. Not somebody I've been with for years now."

"Is that right? So where does that leave me exactly?"

"I'm not sure. But you can't change fate, you know?"

"So, I'm *not* the man of your dreams?"

"Not according to this, you're not."

"Great," scoffed Scott, clearly unimpressed. "So, what does *my* horoscope say?"

Scott was a Scorpio. Gemma scanned down the page and read his horoscope. "Apparently," she said. "Luck is on your side. Hey! Maybe you're gonna win the lottery!"

Scott snorted a laugh. "Yeah? Well, if I do, I'm certainly not giving you a penny."

They both laughed. Gemma thoroughly enjoyed pushing Scott's buttons. He always took things too seriously. They'd been together for over three years now, having met at college. Scott was tall and athletic. It also didn't hurt that he was *fucking fantastic* in bed. Gemma felt that, in another life, they'd have made a great couple; she was slim and sexy and *fucking fantastic* in bed too, even if she did say so herself. Things were a little more complicated these days though…

Gemma's phone rang. She picked it up from the compartment in the centre console and checked the screen.

"It's Bex," she informed Scott.

"Uh oh," said Scott, sarcastically. "I guess we're in trouble. Although, she really should've expected us to be late."

"Exactly!" said Gemma, nodding her head enthusiastically. "And this time, it's not even *my* fault!" They had gotten turned around several miles back. It wasn't until they had noticed signs directing them to some place neither of them had ever even heard of, that they realised they'd made a wrong turn. By that point, they'd already driven a good twelve-or-so miles in the wrong direction. It was no surprise that they were late.

Gemma answered the call. "Hey sexy," she said, smiling cheekily and raising her eyebrows in

Scott's direction. Scott shook his head, focusing on the road once again.

"Hey," replied Bex, her voice breaking a little on the other end of the line. "You're late, as per usual. Where are you guys?"

"Honestly? I have no idea." Gemma chuckled to herself. "We can't be too far now though."

"Tell her we'll probably just be another fifteen minutes or so," Scott interjected.

"About fifteen minutes, Scott says."

"Alright," said Bex. "Well, hurry up then. We're all starting to grow a little impatient here."

"Yeah, yeah. We'll be as quick as we can."

"Alright. See you soon."

"Bye." Gemma hung up the phone and returned it to the slot in the centre console.

"So," said Scott. "*Are* we in trouble?"

Gemma shrugged her shoulders. "Probably," she said. "But they'll get over it. Maybe you should drive a bit slower, make them wait a little longer."

Scott laughed. "You know what? I'm really looking forward to this weekend."

"Of course you are! What's *not* to look forward to? The sun's out. You've got all this fresh air. We'll do some exercise, drink some beer. And you get to do all of that in the company of your gorgeous girlfriend."

Scott laughed. "Aren't I lucky?"

Gemma laughed in return. "You sure are!"

***

Twenty minutes later, Scott drove his car into the car park and parked up next to Joe. Unlike Joe, he wasn't too concerned about the birds shitting on his roof -

his car was a fifteen-year-old Nissan, already on its last legs - so he was quite happy to park directly under the trees.

Abbie was somewhat relieved when they finally arrived. She'd started to think they might not make it. She'd had to spend the last twenty minutes exchanging pleasantries with Mike. Again, she liked Mike. He was a good guy. He was funny and kind, and he wasn't bad looking at all. Perhaps she could even see herself in a relationship with him at some point in the future. She just didn't know if she was ready for that just yet.

"You took your time," said Abbie, as both Gemma and Scott climbed out of the car.

"Yeah," said Scott. "Sorry about that. We took a wrong turn about an hour ago and nearly ended up somewhere entirely different."

"Seriously?" laughed Bex. "That's why you're late? You mean to tell me that Gemma was *actually* ready on time for a change?"

"Hey," said Gemma, feigning upset. "I'm right here, you know."

"I know it's hard to believe," said Scott, pretending as though he couldn't hear Gemma. "But, yes - she was *actually* ready on time today!"

"No way," said Bex, shaking her head. "That's impossible."

"Thanks for the vote of confidence," said Gemma.

They were all laughing now.

Scott moved to the back of his car and popped open the boot. When he returned, he was carrying Gemma's rucksack. "Here you go," he said, holding the bag out at arm's length.

"Thank you," she said, taking it from him and hoisting it onto her back. "I thought you might've offered to carry it for me though."

"Ha! Yeah, well - you thought wrong."

"So, anyway," Abbie called to Scott, as he returned to the car to gather up the last of his belongings. "I'm told you're our fearless leader."

"Apparently so," said Scott. He pulled his own rucksack from the boot of his car and slung it over one shoulder. He then closed the boot and locked the car.

"So, you know where we're going, right?"

"Nope. But I've got a map and directions and some solid recommendations for things to do. Caves to explore, a lake to swim in."

"Well, I guess that's better than nothing. Although, if it's all the same to you, I think I'll pass on the swimming."

Scott shrugged his shoulders. "Fine by me."

"Alright then, leader," said Joe, patting Scott on the back. "Lead the way."

THREE

The battered tarmac road cut a rough path through the woodland. Ragged potholes littered the route. The edges of the road were undefined, the tarmac crumbling away into the undergrowth.

As they walked, Abbie tried her best to keep herself to herself. She breathed in the fresh air, the scent of the forest engulfing her senses. Birds were singing in the trees.

Scott, Joe and Mike were at the front of the group, while Abbie, Bex and Gemma followed from a distance. Bex and Gemma were chatting and laughing about something or other, while Abbie tried her best to focus on the infinite sights and sounds that surrounded her.

Not watching where she was going, suddenly she felt her weight drop beneath her. Her foot dropped into one of the cavernous potholes, her foot twisting awkwardly beneath itself. "Ow! Shit!" moaned Abbie, as her leg bent uncomfortably. A surge of pain rushed through her body.

Everybody stopped. The three lads turned back to see what was happening.

Quickly, Gemma grabbed onto Abbie's arm, preventing her from falling. "You okay?" she said.

"Fuck. No. Not really. I think I sprained my ankle."

Scott, Joe and Mike all jogged back. Mike offered his arm, which Abbie gratefully took a hold of.

"It's not broken, is it?" asked Scott.

"I don't think so," said Abbie. "I'm pretty sure I'd be in a lot more pain if it was." As a child - and through a good proportion of her teens - Abbie had attended dance classes twice per week. As such, she'd twisted her ankle more times than she cared to remember. She was pretty much the expert on what sprained ankles felt like. "Why don't they fix this fucking road?"

"I don't think they're all that bothered," said Joe. "I don't imagine many people walk down here. It's probably just access for the farms. Most likely it's only tractors that drive down here, hence the giant potholes."

"Yeah," scoffed Abbie. "Well, they should fix it anyway."

"Are you alright?" asked Mike. He genuinely sounded concerned. "Do you think you can walk?" He now had one arm under Abbie's armpit and hooked around her waist.

Abbie nodded. "I'm fine," she said, as she untangled herself from Mike's grasp, grateful for his help, but not wanting to give him the wrong impression for too long. "I just need to walk it off."

"That's my girl," said Bex, offering her encouragement.

Abbie couldn't help but laugh.

"Anyway," said Scott, addressing the group. "We'll be off the road in less than a minute, then we won't have to contend with the potholes anymore."

"What do you mean?" asked Joe.

Scott turned and pointed along the road. "Our path through the woods starts right there."

Only now did Abbie notice the fence that ran perpendicular to the road. It was in a terrible state of disrepair. Most of the posts had fallen and had seemingly been reclaimed by the forest. Still, a few of the posts remained upright. A few yards ahead, between two of those posts, a gate hung crooked, the galvanised steel that made up its frame twisted and bent. One of the hinges had been torn off. The other remained in place, although the welds were rusted through.

They approached the gate. Abbie hobbled along, rotating her foot in an attempt to free up her ankle.

At the gate, Scott clambered onto it, standing with his arms wide, like some glorious leader about to address his disciples. "Alright. This is it," he said. "This gate, right here, is the last sign of civilised humanity you're going to see for the next few days. From here on out, it's us versus nature."

Mike burst out in laughter. "Thanks for that," he said, doing his best to contain himself. "How about we just keep moving, yeah?" He then walked around the gate, stepping through an opening to the right, that no doubt used to be blocked by the fence.

Joe and Bex linked arms and followed Mike through. Gemma followed behind them.

As Abbie passed the gate, Scott hopped back down to the ground.

"After you," said Abbie, waving her arms to usher him on.

"No, no," said Scott. "Ladies first."

"Aren't you supposed to be leading the way?"

"I can lead from back here. To be fair, I do most of my best work from behind. Just ask Gemma." He was grinning from ear to ear, clearly pleased with his own joke.

Abbie rolled her eyes. She shook her head. "Oh, God. I guess I asked for that, didn't I?"

"You sure did, Abs," said Scott, draping his arm over Abbie's shoulder and leading her through the gate. "You sure did."

***

The hike was arduous. Abbie hadn't expected it to be quite as tough as it was. The hills around here were steep, and they seemed to stretch infinitely onward, disappearing up and beyond the horizon. Her ankle was holding up well though; at least she had that to be grateful for.

Abbie spent much of the hike taking photographs. She must've taken hundreds of pictures of the scenery, trying to find ways to make the wall of trees look interesting. Her favourite trick was to get low and angle the camera, so that the trees looked to be running diagonally through the frame. Doing so always seemed to make her pictures more dramatic. Once she was home, she'd run the pictures through her editing software, to get the colours to pop.

She had hoped she might be able to get some photographs of the wildlife, but, so far, most of the animals seemed to be camera-shy. There were plenty of birds around, and she had managed to photograph a squirrel, digging up the nuts it had buried some time before.

As difficult as the hike was, everybody still seemed to be having a lot of fun. The canopy above them blocked out a lot of the sunlight, but the air around them remained warm. Despite the uncomfortable humidity, Joe still seemed to have the energy to chase Bex with the dismembered branch of a tree, threatening to tickle her with it, should he catch her. Everybody found this hilarious, even as Bex tumbled to the ground, screaming at the top of her lungs.

Scott had to check the map on a few occasions, just to be sure they were still on track. Not that they had somewhere specific to be, but they still needed to know where they were, so they could find their way to the caves and the lake that some of them were so keen to find.

At one point, they had to cross a stream. Joe went first, scooting down the embankment, before hopping over the water and scrambling up on the other side. He then helped Bex across. Scott, Gemma and Mike followed. Abbie was the last to cross. As she pushed her way up the slope on the far side of the stream, her ankle twinged, threatening to give way. Mike must've seen this; he held out his hand and hoisted her up.

As soon as she was up on the other side, then a deer bolted past, scaring every one of them half to death. Abbie stumbled back and quickly found herself in a sitting position on the ground.

"Jesus-fucking-Christ!" screamed Gemma. "Where the fuck did that thing come from?"

They all laughed. Mike helped Abbie back to her feet.

They must've been walking for around three hours, before Scott finally declared that they had arrived. "This is it," he informed the others. "We should set up camp here." He then slid his bag off his shoulder and dropped it to the ground.

"Here?" said Bex. "Really? We're in the middle of nowhere."

Mike chuckled. "This whole forest is the middle of nowhere."

"Oh, *ye of little faith*," said Scott, groaning as he stretched his arms high above his head. "You really think I'd bring us out into the middle of the woods, with no idea where we're going?" He shook his head, feigning disappointment. "If my navigation skills have served me well - and I'm pretty sure they *will have* - we should be almost dead-centre between the lake and the caves. And besides, we came out here to get away from everything, didn't we?"

"I guess so," said Abbie, dropping her own bag to the forest floor. She sat down beside it, sweeping the ground with her hand, shifting aside a pile of fallen leaves.

Scott draped his arm around Gemma's neck and pulled her in close. He continued - "Besides, it'll be getting dark soon. We don't want to be going much further. We ought to get the tents up while we still have some light."

"You're the boss," said Gemma, sounding unimpressed, stroking Scott's arm before slinking away from him.

"Well," said Joe. "I guess this is as good a spot as any."

"No, no, no," said Scott. "This is the absolute *best* spot. Trust me."

"If you say so, buddy."

Scott crouched beside his bag. He flipped it open, reached inside and pulled out his tent. He then began to assemble the rods that would hold up the canvas.

Abbie followed suit. She pulled open her bag and tipped out the contents. She and Bex then began to pass bits and pieces between themselves, assembling the tent.

"Do you two need a hand?" asked Mike, as he stood over Abbie and Bex.

"Oh… no," said Abbie. "I think we got it. Thank you, though." Abbie felt a little bad for being so abrupt with him, but they *really* didn't need his help - she and Bex were quite capable of pitching their tent by themselves.

"Yeah, we're good," said Bex. "Why don't you go help Joe, since you'll be sharing with him."

"What?" said Joe, looking up from the pile of plastic rods laid out before him. "Me and Mike?"

"Yeah," chuckled Bex, the disappointed look on Joe's face clearly amusing her. "And I'm sharing with Abbie. It's not like *she* can share with Mike, is it? No offence, Mike."

Mike laughed. "None taken. Although I would like to point out that I'm *not* some sort of pervert."

"Yeah? Well, we'll just have to take your word on that, won't we?"

"Okay. Fine. Whatever." Joe began to slide his tent poles through the loops affixed at each corner of the tent. "I don't really care either way. Let's just get these tents up, shall we?"

"Yeah," said Scott. "The sooner we get the tents up, the sooner I can have a beer."

"Fuck it," said Joe, pushing himself up off his knees. "Why wait?" He pulled a bottle of beer from his bag and tossed it to Scott. Scott caught the bottle with one hand, popped it open with his teeth and took a long gulp. Joe then pulled out a second bottle for himself.

"Ahhh," said Scott. "I needed that."

"I didn't know you had a drinking problem," joked Abbie.

"I don't. Not yet, anyway."

Abbie smiled.

"Let's just get it done then," said Gemma, straightening out a ground sheet. "I could do with a drink myself."

"And I thought *I* was the alcoholic?" said Scott, laughing hysterically.

Gemma frowned. She slapped Scott on the arm. They were all laughing now.

Between them, they pitched three tents in the clearing.

FOUR

Mike had gathered a number of branches and built a small fire in the middle of the camp. The three tents had been positioned around the clearing, so that each one opened up in the same direction, towards the fire. Abbie had taken it upon herself to place a number of solar-powered lanterns around the clearing, hanging them from the branches of the trees that surrounded them. The light they emitted was a cool blue, giving the forest an eerie appearance as the sun began to set.

Joe, Mike and Scott were sitting in their foldable camp chairs, right next to the fire. They each had a bottle of beer, from which they were drinking. Bex was crouched beside the fire, roasting a marshmallow over the flames.

Abbie and Gemma were sitting on either side of a small plastic table; the kind that could be folded away to the size of a phone book when not in use. Like the boys, they too were drinking bottled beer. Gemma had brought a pack of cards with her. She was currently busy shuffling them. "So," she asked Abbie. "What are we playing?"

"Whatever," said Abbie, sipping her beer. "Completely up to you."

"Why don't you girls play strip poker?" said Joe, snorting back a laugh. The light of the fire danced over his face, his eyes twinkling from behind heavy shadows.

"Don't be such a pervert, Joe," said Bex. "It's not a good look for you. And besides, maybe you and I can play *that* game later."

"We're not sharing a tent, remember?"

"Oh, yeah. Well, maybe you can play with Mike then."

"No thank you," said Mike, before guzzling the last of his beer. Scott finished his beer too, and tossed the empty bottle aside.

"Poker really isn't my game anyway," said Abbie. "I couldn't tell you what the difference is between a straight and a flush. I'm guessing you'd need to know that in order to play poker, right?"

"Pretty much, yeah." Gemma split the pack of cards, fanned them out, then slid them back inside each other, one half interwoven with the other. "How about we just stick to something simple. Crazy Eights?"

"Sounds good to me."

"Crazy Eights it is." Gemma dealt the cards out as required, then made up the stacks needed to play the game.

Bex removed her marshmallow from the fire, blew on it, then stuffed it into her mouth. She chomped away at it noisily, the melted confectionery causing her tongue to stick to the roof of her mouth.

"So, what's the plan for tomorrow then, Scott," asked Mike.

"Since when did I make the plans?" said Scott, popping open another bottle of beer.

"Since you were designated leader. Besides, you're the only one who actually knows where they're going."

"Right. Fair enough. Well, we could go check out the caves. They're supposed to be pretty *spectacular*." He made jazz-hands, as if the idea that anybody could be impressed by some caves was entirely ridiculous.

Mike laughed. "Sounds good to me."

Abbie placed her last card. "That's it," she said. "I'm out. I win."

"Shit!" complained Gemma, clearly annoyed. She gathered up the cards and reassembled the pack. "Best of three?"

"Sure."

Gemma shuffled the cards once again, then dealt them out. Although they were face down, one of the cards that landed before Abbie looked different to the others - they were all blue, except for this one. Abbie picked this card from the pile. "What's this?" she asked as she turned it over. Immediately, she knew what it was.

"Oh, shit," said Gemma. "How did that get in there?"

It was a tarot card. The picture was of a skeleton, draped in a black cloak; the grim reaper - death itself. In one hand it held a scythe, a drop of blood falling from the point of the blade. With the other hand, it beckoned any onlooker in with one curved, bony finger. At the bottom of the card was the word 'DEATH'.

Gemma laughed. "That's spooky" she said, nonchalantly. But Abbie didn't feel quite so relaxed about it. It was horrible. It made her feel as though death was watching over her. Tarot cards were supposed to be used to predict the future. What if this was some sort of an omen?

"What is it?" said Bex, turning away from the fire, peering over Abbie's shoulder.

"It's the death card," replied Gemma.

"And… What does *that* mean?"

"It means that Abbie is probably going to die tonight."

Gemma was smiling gleefully. Abbie knew that she was joking. Still, that didn't make her feel any less uncomfortable. "Don't say that!" she said. "Did you put it in here?"

"No," chuckled Gemma. "Not on purpose anyway. It must've just got mixed up, that's all."

"Hey," said Scott, sitting forward in his chair and finishing his beer. "That reminds me. I had a story I wanted to tell you guys."

"Oh, God," said Gemma, rolling her eyes. "You're not about to tell the story about *that boy*, are you."

Scott raised an eyebrow. "That's exactly what I'm about to do, yeah."

"What boy?" asked Bex.

It was the same question that had crossed Abbie's mind. She didn't like the sound of this - not one bit. She wasn't sure that she really wanted to hear this story at all.

Scott stood from his chair. He finished his beer, then discarded the bottle into the undergrowth. "Okay," he said excitedly, as if he were about to tell the greatest story ever told. "So, my friend recommended this place. He said it was great for camping. So, I Googled it, and, yeah, there's some really cool stuff to do around here."

Bex sat on Joe's lap. She popped the cap off a bottle of beer using the opener attached to her keychain. She then handed it to Joe, before popping open another for herself.

Gemma gathered up the cards once again and began to shuffle them. Abbie thought that she was barely listening to Scott. Judging by her earlier reaction, she'd already heard this story.

Scott continued - "But then I started diggin' a little deeper. I found out that this area is notorious for people disappearing."

"What do you mean, '*disappearing*'," said Mike. A deep frown was etched to his forehead.

"Disappearing. As in, *disappearing*. Vanished. Here one day, gone the next. It seems to be campers, mostly. They head into the woods for a few days camping, but then they're never heard from again."

Abbie didn't believe a word of what Scott was saying. If she did, she would no doubt have been terrified. But Scott was full of shit. She felt sure he was just trying to scare them. Abbie had watched enough horror movies to not be scared by some cheesy, campfire tale. "And you thought you'd bring *us* here?" she said, sarcastically. "Thanks for that."

"Well, I don't believe that people can just disappear," said Scott. "Do you?"

Abbie simply raised her eyebrows.

"Anyway," said Scott. "There's more."

Mike tipped his head back and groaned. "Not more!"

Abbie couldn't help but feel amused.

"Yes, more. You see, then I started reading rumours about some sort of monster in the woods. Like, some sort of bigfoot."

Bex almost choked on her beer. She spat out a mouthful and laughed. "A bigfoot?"

"Apparently so. People say they've seen it."

"Bullshit!" said Joe, shaking his head.

"Hey, I'm not sayin' *I've* seen it. I'm sayin' a bunch of random people on the internet claim they've seen it. I agree with *you* - it's probably bullshit."

"There's no *probably* about it."

"However…"

"Really?" said Abbie. "You aren't finished yet?"

Scott ignored her. "…I then read about a massacre that *really* did take place here, about twenty years ago."

"Great," said Joe, dripping in sarcasm. He rolled his eyes as he finished the last of his beer.

"There was this kid," said Scott. "A little boy. He wasn't like the other kids. He was a bit retarded. Maybe he had some sort of disfigurement too."

"*Maybe*?" laughed Mike. "Why do I get the impression you're making this up as you go along?"

Scott shook his head, dismissing Mike's doubts (and apparently completely unaware of the disbelieving looks on everybody else's faces). He continued - "His name was Edward Tedstone. People used to call him Teddy. As it turns out, that was quite an apt name, as, being a little slow and less mature than the other kids, he continued playing with his teddy bears all through his childhood."

Gemma dealt out the cards again, still paying little attention to Scott's story.

Scott continued - "So, one day he came down to the woods with his teddy bears, to play. He was just minding his own business, having a teddy bears' picnic, when a bunch of bigger kids showed up. They liked to pick on Teddy 'cause he was different. They decided to mess up his game. Then one of them hit him, for no reason whatsoever. That was when Teddy snapped."

Abbie could picture the scene, playing out in her mind, as if she were watching a movie - a small, timid boy - Teddy - minding his own business, playing with his favourite teddy bears; a group of older boys - teenagers, perhaps - much bigger than him, approaching through the woods; the teenagers towering over the boy, looking down on him, berating him; one of the teenagers stomping through his toys, kicking them carelessly aside; the boy, trying to stop them, knocked to the ground; one of the teenagers - the biggest and scariest of the gang - balling his fists; the little boy, crawling through the dirt, scrambling to protect his precious teddies; the fist, cracking into the side of the little boy's jaw.

Suddenly, Abbie found herself feeling a little less comfortable.

Scott continued - "Teddy took a knife…"

"Where did he get a knife?" interrupted Bex. It seemed clear to Abbie, that Bex didn't believe a word of it.

"I don't know. Maybe he took it there as part of his game. Anyway, he got a knife and then he stabbed all the kids to death."

Abbie wasn't sure if she believed Scott's story or not, but her heart was racing now. True or not, the story was starting to scare her.

"Once they were all dead," said Scott. "He chopped their bodies into little bits. By the time the police got there, Teddy was gone. All they found was the pieces of the kids, served up to the teddy bears on little plastic plates."

Abbie could see it. Several teddies sitting around the edge of a picnic blanket. Before them were human body parts, sitting on a child's multicoloured tableware. A stuffed rabbit sat before a pile of human eyeballs. A brown dog with ragged, chewed ears sat before a severed hand, the flesh peeled from the fingers. A grey bear - one of the plastic eyes missing, its fur matted - sat before a heart, blood pooling on the plate and cascading over the rim.

"It was like some grotesque teddy bear's picnic," said Scott, wrapping up his story.

Abbie didn't know what to make of the story. Everybody else seemed to be entirely nonplussed about it. But Abbie could help the sense of dread building inside her. Suddenly, she felt exhausted.

"Yawn!" said Gemma, clearly not as ill affected as Abbie had been. "I told you it was bullshit."

"Yeah?" said Scott. "How the fuck would you know?"

"It would've been on the news."

"It was twenty years ago!"

Gemma shrugged her shoulders, apparently disinterested in discussing it any further. "I still say it's bullshit."

"Where did you read this, Scott?" asked Joe.

"On the internet," said Scott

Mike snorted half a laugh. "It's *definitely* true then!" he said, dripping in sarcasm.

"Yeah... Well... Whatever. I thought it was a cool story anyway." Scott turned and dropped into one of the camp chairs. He slumped back and popped open another beer.

Gemma picked up a stack of cards and offered them to Abbie. "So," she said. "We playin', or what?"

Abbie shook her head. She didn't think she'd be able to play, even if she'd wanted to; her brain felt scrambled. She couldn't help but think about that boy. What if the story *was* true? What had happened to that boy? Did they ever find him? "I don't think so," she said. "I'm not in the mood anymore. I think I just need to get some sleep."

"You okay?" asked Mike, sitting forward in his chair, a genuine look of concern on his face.

"Yeah," Abbie lied. "I'm fine."

"Scott's story didn't creep you out, did it?" said Gemma. "He *is* full of crap, you know?"

Scott shook his head. "I'm telling you, now - that really happened!"

"Whatever," said Gemma, rolling her eyes.

Abbie forced herself to smile. "I'm fine, honestly. I'm just tired. I'm gonna hit the sack." She stood and headed for her tent.

"I'm coming too," said Bex. She kissed Joe, before standing and following Abbie into the tent.

"Yeah," said Scott. "Maybe we should all get some sleep. We've got a busy day tomorrow."

"Sounds like a good idea," agreed Mike.

Everybody headed for their respective tents. Gemma crawled into her tent. Scott was about to follow her in, when Joe stopped him.

"Should we put the fire out?" asked Joe.

"It'll be fine," said Scott. "Just leave it."

"We won't cause a forest fire or nothin'?"

"No. It's fine. It'll go out by itself at some point." Scott then climbed into his tent and zipped it shut. Immediately, he and Gemma began giggling.

"Oh, great," said Abbie leaning out of the tent, rolling her eyes.

"Yeah," said Joe. "Good luck getting to sleep tonight." He spoke loudly so that Gemma and Scott would hear, no doubt hoping that the realisation that they could be heard might put them off any furious lovemaking they had planned.

Abbie scoffed. "Great. Thanks. Well, goodnight."

"Goodnight."

Abbie zipped up the tent, climbed into her sleeping bag and closed her eyes, trying to sleep through the sound of Bex's gentle snoring. It seemed to take forever for Abbie to finally drift off.

At least Gemma and Scott decided *not* to inflict the sounds of their lovemaking on the others. Gemma must've refused Scott's advances. At least she had that to be grateful for.

FIVE

Marie was pissed off. It was late. It was dark. And they were driving through the middle of fucking nowhere. And now, to top it all off, her phone signal had dropped out once again. "Shit!" she complained, as the green arrow that followed the path displayed on her screen blinked to red. She was just about ready to give up.

"What's wrong?" asked Jim, from his place behind the steering wheel.

The car was cruising along the country road, the headlights offering little in the way of illumination, thanks to the thick trees that seemed to surround them in every direction. The road twisted and curved, cutting through dense forest. Should a car appear from around the corner, travelling in the opposite direction, there was every chance the two drivers wouldn't see each other. Then they might crash. Marie was glad it wasn't her who was driving. Thankfully, what with it being as late as it was, there weren't many other cars on the road. "The signal's gone again."

"Don't worry," said Jim, clearly unconcerned about the fact that they were lost. "We're on this road for a while. I'm sure this is the right direction. I'm sure your signal will be back by the time we need it."

Marie shook her head. "I just don't get why it keeps going."

"Babe," chuckled Jim. "We're in the middle of nowhere."

"There's no such thing as '*the middle of nowhere*' nowadays. It's impossible to get lost. You can get phone signal literally everywhere."

"Clearly not."

Marie rolled her eyes. "Yeah, but you know what I mean. We *should* have a signal out here."

"But we don't. There's nothing we can do about that, so stop worrying about it. It's fine. We're not lost."

Marie could feel herself frowning. "You could've fooled me. If we're not lost, then where in the fuck are we?"

Jim opened his mouth to speak, but when no words came, that was when Marie understood that there was no reasonable answer for him to give. Instead, he just shrugged his shoulders.

Marie turned her attention back to the phone. The display at the top of the screen still showed no bars. Still no service. The silence lasted for all of two minutes, before Jim decided to speak once again.

"Besides," said Jim. "We're only out here because of you. It was your parents who decided to move out to the middle of nowhere."

"That's not my fault, is it?" Marie could feel her annoyance growing. Jim's snarkiness was the last thing she needed right now. And he needed to concentrate on the road.

"No. But it was you who wanted to come visit."

"What do you want me to do? Never see them again?"

"Would that really be so bad?"

Marie stared daggers into Jim. She could practically taste the disgust oozing from her.

Jim smiled. "Oh, relax," he said, giggling. "I'm just kidding. It's fine. Stop worrying about the bloody sat nav."

Marie shook her head. She returned her gaze to her phone. The truth was, Jim was right. It was *her* parents who had moved out here. It was *she* who had wanted to come see them. They were retired now, and they were following their dream of moving out to the country. But now they were so far away that Marie couldn't see them every week, as she previously had. In fact, this was only the second time they'd been out there since her parents had moved. That was over a year ago now, and she missed them terribly.

The arrow on her screen blinked from red to green, jumped forward a few miles, then once again began to track their position on the marked route. "I don't believe it. We've got a signal again."

"Well, there you go," said Jim, as if this sudden development was all down to him. "Problem solved. Nothing to worry about."

No sooner had Jim finished talking, then the car jerked forward as a loud *thunk* emanated from somewhere under the bonnet. A crunching whir buzzed from the chassis and the engine began to chug.

"What was that?" said Marie, a sudden sense of panic embedding itself into her soul.

"I don't know," said Jim. The way he shifted through the gears and stamped on the pedals told Marie that the car was all but dead.

"But it *was* the car, right?"

"*Obviously.* That noise didn't come from me, did it?"

Marie ignored his sarcasm. "Well, what is it? What's happening?"

"I don't know." Slowly, the car rolled along the road until finally it spluttered and ground to a halt. Thin plumes of smoke rolled out from each side of the bonnet. "Fuck."

Through the front window, the headlights illuminated a small section of the road, where a sharp corner turned off and split a cluster of trees in two. The trees ahead seemed to be set out in neat, orderly rows; the first row was lit up by the yellow glow of the car's lights; the row behind was duller, especially where the harsh shadows from the front row fell upon them; the row behind that one - and every row beyond - was pitch black.

Marie suddenly felt alone. Jim was sat by her side, of course, but other than him, there would be nobody else around here for miles. "Is that it?" she said, forcing herself to keep her voice in check. "Is it dead?"

"Dead as a fuckin' dormouse," said Jim. He slammed the palm of his hand against the wheel, rattling the steering column. "Shit!"

"Should we call the AA?"

Jim tipped his head back and took a breath. He then looked at Marie. "Do you have any signal?"

Marie checked her phone. For the briefest of moments, her heart stopped beating. "No."

Jim sighed. "Well," he groaned, sounding as if he were in some kind of physical pain. "We might have to walk it then?"

Marie felt her nose crinkle. Was he fucking insane? Had he completely lost it? They couldn't walk anywhere. Not now. Not out here. Not in the middle of the fucking night. "What? Nope. Fuck that."

"You got any better ideas?"

"Can't you fix it?"

Jim snorted, puffed out his chest, shook his head and shrugged his shoulders, all at the same time. His eyebrows were lowered as he looked to Marie, directing his annoyance in her direction. But this wasn't her fault, was it? She didn't cause his piece-of-shit car to break down. "How should I know?" he said, disgruntled. "But I'll take a look if it'll make you happy."

"It might be something simple," said Marie, trying to remain optimistic - not that she felt that way inside.

"Yeah. Maybe." Jim reached down past his knees and pulled the lever to pop open the bonnet. He then leaned over Marie's lap, pulled open the glove box and retrieved a Mini Maglite from inside.

"That's a bit small, isn't it?" said Marie.

"Size isn't everything."

"You keep telling yourself that," said Marie, trying to inject some levity to the situation. Jim didn't seem keen to play along. He rolled his eyes and climbed out of the car.

Marie watched through the windscreen as Jim rounded the car. He clicked on the torch and held it between his teeth, before lifting the bonnet, blocking him from Marie's view.

Marie slumped back in her seat. She closed her eyes and imagined herself somewhere else. This wasn't how she'd hoped to be spending her Friday night. They should've been at her parents hours ago. She'd spoken to her mother not long before they'd set off - her mother had told her she was cooking a beef stew, and that there would be plenty left for them when they arrived. It was only then that Marie realised she was starving; her tummy grumbled, making her almost feel sick.

She opened her eyes and looked at her phone. Much to her surprise, she found she had signal once again. "Hey!" she called, her voice drifting out the open driver's side window. "Phone's working! Should we call someone?"

Jim didn't respond.

Marie raised her eyebrows. Had he not heard her? Or was he just being an arsehole and ignoring her for no good reason?

"Jim? You hear me? Can you fix it, or should I phone the mechanic?"

Still nothing.

"Jim?"

Marie tucked her phone into her jeans pocket and climbed out of the car. Slowly, cautiously, she approached the front of the car.

Jim wasn't there.

Or, more precisely, not *all* of Jim was there.

The miniature LED torch sat in a pool of blood. In the darkness, the blood looked black, except for where the beam of light spilled from the end of the silver cylinder; there, the blood was bright crimson.

Marie's mouth dropped open, her eyes fixed on the blood, the cogs of her brain whirring, trying to figure out just what she was seeing. For a moment, she squeezed her eyes tight shut. When she opened them, they had made their way to the engine bay. There, Jim's hands were still gripping the head of the engine, no longer attached to his body. The right hand had been severed at the wrist, the flesh ragged where it looked to have been torn away. The left hand was separated halfway along the forearm, the skin lacerated, both the radius and ulna bones snapped like twigs and protruding from the haggard meat, blood dripping from the jagged points, into the engine of the car.

Marie's heart flipped upside-down and tore itself in two. She didn't want to scream - whoever had done this to Jim, maybe they didn't realise she was there; her screams would only serve to alert them to her presence, to call them back to her. So, she held her breath and tried desperately to force her body not to vomit. She ran back to the passenger seat and jumped in. She pulled her phone from her pocket and checked for signal.

There were still two bars displayed at the tip of the screen. For the briefest of moments, she felt a sense of hope trickle into her being. She opened up the keypad on her phone and began to dial.

The window beside her head shattered. Shards of glass flew into the car, stinging Marie like a thousand nettles. One of the larger shards sliced open her cheek. The blood felt warm as it trickled down to her chin.

Marie screamed then. She dropped her phone, watching as it tumbled into the driver's side footwell, far out of her reach.

She felt a hand grab a hold of her hair, pulling it so taught that she felt it may be ripped from her scalp. And then she was being dragged backwards out of the car, through the broken window, the glass that remained within the steel frame shredding her t-shirt and slicing through her back like razor blades.

She hit the rough tarmac hard. She tried to break her fall, but this only led to her hand twisting beneath her own body, bending back to the point that she was sure she felt at least one of the tendons pop. She wanted to scream then too, but with her lungs expelled of all their air, the best she could manage was a light whimper.

Marie tried to push herself up, but a heavy foot slammed down on the back of her neck, shoving her face down into the tarmac, cracking her two front teeth clean in half. She could taste blood now.

From the corner of her eye, her vision blurred, Marie watched as a dark shape moved to tower over her. She couldn't see what it was holding in its hand. It looked like some kind of thin implement, curved at one end, jutting off at an angle. And then she recognised it - it was a hammer.

The first blow landed at the back of her head, right behind the ear. A loud *crack* flooded her entire being. She felt her skull shatter. Her brain melted, as if it had been doused in sulphuric acid.

The second blow landed on the temple, shattering the orbital bone, the splattered eyeball leaking from the socket, just about hanging on by the ocular nerve.

Marie didn't feel the third blow land. Nor the fourth. Nor the fifth, or the sixth, or the seventh. Had she been counting, she'd have counted a total of twelve blows with the hammer, which eventually turned her entire head into a pile of broken bone and mashed brain, every drop of blood evacuating her body.

But to Marie, that no longer mattered. She was dead now. Nothing else would matter to her ever again.

SIX

The campfire was still smouldering when Joe emerged from his tent. He hadn't checked the time, but it was still dark. It couldn't have been any earlier than 3:00a.m. But he was desperate for a piss, his bladder full from all the beer he'd drank the previous evening.

He had pulled on his shorts, but had decided against his t-shirt. He regretted that somewhat; despite how gloriously warm the previous day had been, a chill now hung in the air. A light mist seemed to swirl around the trees, no doubt waiting to drop its summer due onto the waiting leaves. Joe rubbed his arms. He could quite easily turn and grab a t-shirt from inside the tent, but right now, that seemed like it would require too much effort. He needed to go drain the lizard, then get back to sleep.

Joe looked over his shoulder, into the tent. Mike was still fast asleep. Carefully, watching where he was planting his feet, Joe began to creep away from the camp, between the trees.

He didn't need to go far. Everybody else was still tucked up in their sleeping bags, so there would be nobody around to get offended at him relieving himself so close by. Still, he passed beyond the first row of trees, just to be safe.

A few steps onward, Joe stopped. He pulled down the front of his shorts, took his dick in hand and began to urinate on a tree. Steam rose from the stream of pee as it spattered from the trunk. It felt good. That uncomfortable feeling in his stomach began to fade.

There was noise. A bush somewhere off to his right rattled. Joe looked back over his shoulder. From this position, he could just about make out the tents in the darkness. But there was nobody there.

It must've just been the wind.

But there it was again. Another noise, closer this time. Rustling leaves and snapping twigs. *An animal, perhaps?*

Spooked, Joe squeezed his abdominal muscles, hoping to squeeze the last of the piss out of his bladder, wringing it dry like a used dishcloth. As soon as he was finished, he shook the last drips from the end of his penis, then tucked it back into his boxers.

He turned back to camp.

There was somebody there, standing right before him. Scott's stomach felt as though it turned inside out. He could taste his heart beating in his throat. For the briefest of moments, he imagined it to be some sort of a monster; a savage beast, ready and willing to tear his throat out. Perhaps it was the bigfoot from Scott's story? No - *much too small*. Quickly, he realised exactly who he was looking at.

"Hey," said Gemma, whisper quiet.

Scott jumped back involuntarily, away from what his body had instinctively perceived to be a threat. "Jesus Christ," he said, keeping his voice hushed. "You scared the shit out of me."

Gemma giggled quietly. "Don't be such a pussy," she said, a wide, twisted grin on her face. She then pushed in close to Joe, placing her hands flat on his bare chest. She tiptoed up and kissed him, long and passionate.

Joe made no effort to prevent this from happening. Instead, he slid his tongue into Gemma's mouth. She tasted good. Then he pulled away. "We can't do this," he said. "Not here."

"Why not?"

Joe raised his eyebrows. "*Why not*? Because *your* boyfriend - who is supposed to be a good friend of mine - and *my* girlfriend - who is supposed to be a good friend of yours - are both asleep, right there," - he pointed back toward the tents - "about five meters away from us. That's *why not*."

Gemma took his hand in both of hers and lowered it. "So?"

"So, I don't really want either of them finding out like this. We need to do this properly." Joe and Gemma had been in a relationship for over two months now. It had just sort-of happened. They'd always been good friends; it just developed from there. Joe never meant to cheat on Bex, but their relationship had really hit a sour spot. They hardly talked anymore, and it seemed to Joe that sex with Bex was completely off the table.

"I've had enough of all the sneaking around," said Gemma. "I need to tell Scott, sooner rather than later."

Joe nodded sincerely. He wanted that too. "Okay. We'll tell them once we're back home. Not here."

"Alright. But *as soon* as we get home. I don't want to be with Scott anymore. I want you." As she said this, her finger slid beneath the waistband of his shorts and found their way to his flaccid penis. She wrapped her hand around it and began to stroke it gently.

Scott felt his cock starting to stiffen. "Okay. As soon as we're home."

"You promise?"

"I promise."

"Good." Gemma pulled her hand out of Joe's shorts, leaving his erection held in place by the elastic, pressed against his belly. Joe had been the one who had said *'not here'*, but as Gemma had begun to stimulate him, he'd quickly changed his mind on the subject. Now, as Gemma had turned back to camp, he found himself entirely disappointed. "Best get back," said Gemma, as she crept through the trees. "Before anybody notices we're gone."

As she walked away, she lifted the oversized t-shirt she was wearing, so that Joe could take a good look at her pert, firm buttocks. She was such a tease.

Joe decided to wait for a moment, just in case anybody had woken. At least if he and Gemma arrived back at camp separately, they could plead their innocence. They could just say that they had both needed to relieve themselves, and that neither of them was even aware that the other was out there.

Something rustled in the trees once again. Joe couldn't see anything. He decided to ignore it and headed back to his tent.

***

Abbie took a long gulp of the water, swilled it, then spit out a mouthful of frothy, minty-fresh toothpaste. The white foam splattered the grass, infused with a healthy dollop of phlegm. It was fairly undignified, brushing one's teeth while camping. But regardless of this, it was still something that needed to be done.

It was morning and Abbie was the first to wake. She had climbed out of her tent to find the fire still billowing a thin trail of smoke into the sky. She had taken herself off between the trees so that she could pee. Then she'd brushed her teeth. When she had returned, she had found Mike to now be awake. He was prodding the fire with a dried piece of wood, hoping to spark the kindling back to life.

He looked up as Abbie emerged from the woods. "Oh," he said. "Good morning. I didn't realise anybody else was up."

"Yeah," said Abbie, stretching her hands to the sky. "Well, I think I beat you to it."

"How did you sleep?"

"Fine, thanks. You?"

"Yeah. About the same." The branch Mike was holding suddenly caught alight. He stuffed it into the fire, beneath the already burned wood, before piling on more dried twigs. The campfire coughed up a plume of white smoke, then began to burn nicely. "There we go. Now we can cook breakfast."

"Did somebody say breakfast?" called a voice from inside one of the tents. It was Scott. "I'd kill for a bacon and egg sandwich."

Mike laughed to himself. "I've got spaghetti. Will that do?"

"Ughh…" said Scott, as he emerged from his tent. " I guess it'll have to, won't it?"

Mike set up a saucepan over the fire, cracked open a can of spaghetti hoops and poured the contents into the pan. While Mike warmed up the pasta, the rest of the campers scrambled from their tents, like beautiful butterflies emerging from their cocoons. Except that, in the cold light of the morning, Abbie couldn't imagine calling any one of her group '*beautiful*' - herself included.

Joe climbed out of his tent first. He stretched his arms out wide and yawned. Bex climbed out of the tent just behind him. Immediately, she wrapped her arms around his waist and leant in to kiss him. Joe grunted and turned his head away. "Uhh… don't," he complained. "At least let me brush my teeth first."

"Don't worry about it," said Bex. "I love your stinky breath."

Joe scoffed. "Well, I don't love *yours*."

Mike distributed the spaghetti hoops into several small, plastic bowls. He then handed them out. Bex stood over Mike, peering over his shoulder. "Can we boil some water?" she asked. "I'd love a cup of tea."

"Comin' right up," said Mike.

Abbie slouched back into her chair, allowing her body to slump down until she was practically horizontal. "Oh, man," she groaned, twisting her head from side to side until the crick in her neck popped. "I slept like a log last night. I was asleep as soon as my head hit the pillow."

"Yeah, me too," said Bex.

"I guess that's what the fresh air does to you," said Mike. With the water boiled, he made a cup of tea and handed it to Bex. "Anybody else want one?" he asked.

"No, thank you," said Abbie, sitting up in the chair, eating her pasta.

Gemma scrambled out of her tent. Her hair was bunched up into a messy bun, the bobble having fallen loose during the night. She stood, yawning, her mouth hanging wide. "Good morning," she said, sucking in a deep breath.

"Morning," Abbie and Bex said simultaneously.

Scott followed Gemma out of the tent. He was wearing nothing other than his boxer shorts. He stood and straightened them out. "We got anything to eat?" he asked.

Mike held out a bowl of spaghetti. Scott grunted as he took it, apparently disappointed. Still, he began to eat.

"So, Scott," said Joe, sitting back in his chair. "As the leader of our little gang, what's the itinerary for today?"

Scott snorted and shrugged his shoulders. "The sun's shining. We've got a map. We've got a compass. Let's just see where the day takes us?"

"Seriously?" said Mike. "Surely we need some sort of a plan."

"Well, what do *you* want to do today?"

Before Mike could answer, Gemma interjected. "I don't care what anybody else is doing today," she said. "*I'm* going swimming."

"I'm really not up for swimming today," said Abbie, very much hoping that she might be able to sway the others. If not, she'd be spending her day sitting on the edge of a lake, topping up her tan. Not that that sounded like such a terrible idea, truth be told.

"Don't be so grumpy, Little Miss Grumpy Pants," said Gemma, bursting with laughter, clearly thinking she was funnier than she actually was.

"I'm not being grumpy. I just don't want to."

"Well, me and Scott are going swimming, aren't we?" She turned her attention to Scott, the tone of her voice instructing him that this was, in actual fact, what they were doing, whether he liked it or not.

"It certainly looks that way," said Scott, rolling his eyes.

"I'll take a walk to the caves with you, if you like," Mike told Abbie.

"Thanks," said Abbie, offering him a wide smile. It was nice of him to offer to keep her company. She imagined Mike may well have wanted to go swimming too. The fact that he'd give that up for her told her that he must really like her.

"We can *all* go to the caves," said Bex.

Gemma shook her head. "Nope. Me and Scott are going swimming. I already told you that."

"Well, it looks like it's just you two."

"Fine by me," said Scott. "That means we can go skinny dipping."

"Like the rest of us being there would stop you from getting your dick out," laughed Joe.

Scott laughed too and nodded his head. "Yeah. That's very true."

"Okay. So that's settled," said Gemma. "The cool kids are going swimming, while the boring kids are going to the caves."

"Whatever makes you happy," said Bex.

"Okay," said Scott, standing from his chair and tipping the last remnants of spaghetti sauce into the flames of the campfire, causing it to hiss. "I'm glad we got that sorted."

SEVEN

The sun was blazing overhead again. The sweltering heat was almost unbearable.

Abbie packed twelve bottles of beer and four bottles of water into her rucksack before heaving it up onto her back. She knew the others would want to drink the beer, but she felt sure that the water - with the weather being as hot as it was - would also be welcomed. The straps of her bag felt tight around her shoulders, and the weight of the contents felt as though it might just weigh her down. But it was nothing she couldn't handle.

Still, Mike offered to help. "You okay with that?" he asked.

"Yeah," Abbie confirmed. "I got it."

Gemma was sitting on one of the chairs, slathering sunscreen onto her legs. She was wearing a pair of denim shorts, the legs barely long enough to cover her snatch. The top half of her body was naked, other than the colourful, striped bikini top she was wearing. Abbie had to admit that Gemma had an incredible body; her skin was tight and smooth, her c-cup breasts were bouncy and pert, her tight abs were visible under the non-existent layer of fat that covered her stomach. "Hey, babe?" asked Gemma. "Can you put some cream on my shoulders?"

"Sure thing," said Scott, taking the bottle from Gemma. He stood behind her, squirted a blob of the sunscreen into the palm of his hand, then began to rub it into her neck and shoulders. Gemma closed her eyes and tipped her head back, enjoying the massage she was receiving.

Abbie noticed that Joe was staring at Gemma, naughty thoughts running through his mind, no doubt. Joe was with Bex; he loved her more than anything. So, quite why he was staring at Gemma, Abbie didn't understand.

Then again, who could blame him. She was beautiful and she was half naked.

Scott must've seen Joe staring too. "You checkin' out my girlfriend?" he said, snapping Joe's attention away from Gemma. A series of deep valleys lined Scott's furrowed brow.

"What?" said Joe, sounding as guilty as sin. "No. I just…"

Then Scott was laughing. "I'm kidding. I don't mind you looking. Gemma likes the attention anyway, don't you?"

Gemma raised her eyebrows. "Fuck off," she said, pulling away from Scott. She stood, her hands on her hips. "Maybe I'm not quite the whore you think I am."

"Yes you are!" smirked Scott. "And that's why I love you!"

Bex emerged from her own tent just a few moments later. Like Gemma, she too wore only a bikini tip and her short shorts. Suddenly, Abbie felt completely overdressed, in her knee length khakis and her plain, white t-shirt. "Right," said Bex. "Are we ready to go?"

"You're gonna need this," said Scott, offering something to Mike. It wasn't until Mike accepted it, that Abbie realised it was a compass.

"Oh, man," said Mike. "I haven't used a compass in years."

"It's easy," said Scott, a patronising tone to his voice. "The arrow always points to North."

"I know how a compass works, dickhead. I just haven't used one in years."

"Yeah, well… You're heading West. Just keep going straight and you eventually come to the caves. Okay?"

"Yeah, yeah. I got it."

"Can we get going, then?" Gemma said, impatiently.

"One second," said Scott. He filled his rucksack with bottles of beer, then took a folded blanket from inside the tent and stuffed it inside. "Okay. Let's go."

"Enjoy your swimming," said Bex.

"We will," replied Gemma.

"I hope the water's really cold."

"Thanks!" said Gemma, her voice light and chirpy, and layered thick with sarcasm. She and Scott then held hands and skipped away between the trees.

"Right," said Mike. "Let's make a move."

***

Joe and Mike rambled through the woods, while Abbie and Bex trailed behind. Mike looked back over his shoulder. "How's it goin' back there?" he asked. "You guys keepin' up?"

"I think we're doing okay," replied Abbie, smiling.

As soon as Mike had returned his gaze to whatever was ahead, Bex leaned into Abbie. 'Well?' she said. "What do you think?"

"About what?" said Abbie, frowning as if she didn't know what Bex was referring to.

"Mike, of course! He clearly fancies the pants off you!"

Bex was keeping her voice down. Abbie really hoped Mike wouldn't hear; if he did, she might just die of embarrassment. "No he doesn't," she said.

"Oh, *please*!" laughed Bex. "He clearly does. You know it. And you like him too!"

"Is that so?" Abbie rolled her eyes.

"Yeah!" The enthusiasm pouring out of Bex was admirable. She wanted Abbie and Mike to get together more than Abbie did herself.

Abbie chuckled to herself. "Yeah, I like him. But just as a friend. I don't fancy him."

"You sure?"

"I'm sure."

Bex contorted her face into a look of disappointment. "Well, why not? He's not *that* bad looking."

"Why don't you date him then?" smirked Abbie.

"Nope. I'm quite happy with *'average'* Joe, thank you very much."

The two girls burst out into a fit of laughter.

Ahead, Joe and Mike both looked back, confused looks etched to their faces. "What's so funny?" asked Joe.

"None of your business," said Bex, poking her tongue out at him.

"Oh. So it's like that, huh?"

"Yep," giggled Bex. "Anyway - are you sure we're goin' in the right direction? I'd have thought we'd been there by now." She and Abbie walked quicker, catching up to the boys.

"Yes. I'm ninety-nine percent sure that this is the right direction."

"Well, it best be. If we get lost out here, it'll be all your fault."

Joe laughed. "We're not gonna get lost. I've got Scott's compass, remember?" He held up the plastic compass by the red and white lace that had been looped through the hole in the top.

"Great," scoffed Bex. "Very reassuring."

Joe draped his arm around Bex's neck and kissed her on the side of the head. Abbie couldn't help but smile. She hoped she could have a relationship like that again someday. Maybe she could have that with Mike. He *was* a good guy. Maybe he was boyfriend material after all.

Abbie returned her focus to the path ahead. "Whoa!" she said, quickly jutting out both her arms in effort to stop the others from walking head on into the strands of barbed wire strung out before them. Somebody had planted a series of stakes into the ground, around five feet apart. Five rows of barbed wire had been strung between them, the top one at around waist height, the bottom one down by Abbie's ankles. The wires between the top and bottom had been evenly spaced. The wire itself was rusty, the savage points corroded due to the years outside. This makeshift barbed wire fence stretched off to the left and disappeared into the trees. The same to the right. It was as if someone had tried to enclose this area of the forest.

"What the hell is this?" said Mike, a rhetorical question, asked of nobody in particular.

"Look," said Joe, pointing off to the right.

Abbie followed his line of sight, to where a scrap of wood had been nailed to one of the posts. Written on the scrap of wood, in a thick, child-like scrawl, were the words 'KEEP OUT'.

"Oh… What the in the *actual* fuck?" said Bex. For a moment, she actually sounded scared. "Who would've put this here. Surely nobody *lives* out here."

"Maybe it's just some sort of joke," said Joe.

"If it is," said Abbie. "Then it's not very funny. This is dangerous - somebody could get hurt. Clearly *somebody* doesn't want anybody coming out here."

"Well - like Bex just said - nobody lives out here. It's not like we're trespassing on private property."

"What if there's a marijuana farm back there?" mused Bex. "You hear about them being found out in the middle of nowhere."

"What? So gangsters put this sign up? I doubt that somehow. But if it just so happens that they did, then we'll just buy an ounce or two, and be on our way." Joe laughed to himself, a sentiment not taken up by the others.

Mike shook his head, knocking his thoughts into order. "I'm sure it's fine. This sign is ancient. Whoever put it here, they're probably long gone."

"You think so." asked Abbie.

"Yeah, I do."

Abbie nodded, agreeing with herself that there was no point in turning back. "Alright," she said. "Let's keep going then. I don't want to hang around here any longer than we have to."

"Alright," said Joe. He placed his knee onto the second row of wire from the top, delicately directing it between two of the barbs, and pushed down. He then wrapped his fingers around the top wire - again, steering well clear of the barbs - and pulled it up. "Ladies first."

Bex went first. She stepped her left leg through first, then slowly inched her head and body through. Once they were clear, she then brought her right leg through. She made it look easy.

Abbie went next, copying the exact movement that had gotten Bex through successfully. She took it slower, but soon enough she was on the other side of the fence, without a scratch on her.

Mike stepped forward. "You wanna go next," he asked Joe.

"No," said Joe. "I got it. Just go."

Mike ducked under the wire.

Joe then released the wire and lifted away his knee. The two wires *twanged* back to their original positions, the sudden movement causing all the wires, along the entire length of the fence, to rattle noisily. Joe then stepped forward and pushed the top wire downwards.

"You're goin' over it?" squealed Bex, her voice jumping two octaves.

"Yeah," said Joe. "I've got long legs." He then lifted his left leg over the top row of barbed wire. To

Abbie, those barbs looked dangerously close to his skin.

"Try not to chop your dick off."

Joe ignored Bex and swung his right leg over. As he did so - and as could have been so easily predicted - he caught the side of his calf on one of the barbs. "Shit!" he said, as he lowered his foot to the ground. He bent to inspect the cut on his leg.

It wasn't bad. It was a small puncture wound, nothing too horrific. A small trickle of blood ran down towards his ankle. Most importantly, he wasn't going to die - unless he caught tetanus, of course, but he wouldn't know about that for quite some time.

"Oh, poor baby," said Bex, jutting out her bottom lip, acting as if she was really concerned. "Do you need to go to the hospital?"

"Nah," said Joe, not quite grasping the sarcasm in Bex's voice. He pressed on the wound, then wiped the blood away with his thumb. "I'll be okay."

"Count yourself lucky," said Mike. "It could've been a lot worse."

"Okay," said Bex. "If we're sure you're not about to die from blood loss, shall we keep moving?"

They continued on through the woods. Abbie couldn't help but look back at the barbed wire and wonder who had actually put it there. Had they put themselves in danger by crossing that barrier? Joe was right, of course; nobody *actually* owned this land. Not legally, anyway. But the law often failed to stop people taking ownership of something that didn't belong to them. What if there were people here who really wouldn't appreciate them trespassing on *their* land? What would they do?

Teddy Bears Picnic

    Abbie could only hope that she would never need to find out.

EIGHT

Gemma kicked up leaves as she walked, dragging her toes through the fallen vegetation that littered the ground. Scott walked alongside her. For the most part, their trek through woods had so far gone by in silence. "You know what?" said Gemma, hoping to spark a conversation.

"What?" asked Scott.

"When we get home, I'm gonna need you to take me out for a nice, juicy steak." That was the best she could come up with; but everyone loves talking about food, don't they?

"A steak?" chuckled Scott. "We've only been out here for one day. How is it that you could possibly be craving a steak right now?"

Gemma frowned. "Are you telling me you wouldn't love a steak right now? Medium-rare, with peppercorn sauce. Chips. Onion rings. Maybe some peas on the side."

"Oooh, yeah," said Scott, swinging Gemma around and pulling her into himself, so that she was forced to walk backwards. "That sounds good to me." He then kissed her, long and deep.

As they kissed, Gemma thought of Joe. He'd be jealous if he could see them now - and the thought pleased her greatly. It could've been *him* that she was kissing right now, but *he* had dragged his heels in telling Bex about their relationship. He didn't want to hurt Bex's feelings. Well - nor did Gemma; she and Bex had been friends since middle school. But if it came to Bex's happiness or her own, she knew which side her bread was buttered on. Gemma knew that she ought to feel guilty - both for kissing Scott right now, *and* for cheating on Scott with Joe - but she didn't; she'd long since gotten over it.

Gemma peeled her lips from Scott's. She looked into his eyes. He was still very handsome. Sure, they'd drifted apart over that last year or so, but that didn't stop her from finding him attractive. Gemma bit her lower lip. Scott was grinning like a maniac. He looked like a big kid.

"Come with me," Gemma whispered seductively, hooking her fingers over the waistband of Scott's shorts and dragging him over to where a fallen oak laid between the trees.

There, Gemma hopped up so that she was sitting on the horizontal trunk. She then pulled Scott in close, hooking her legs around his waist, pulling their hips together. They kissed again, her hands pushing the rucksack from his shoulders, so that it dropped to the floor, then sliding up under his t-shirt, lifting it up and over his head. She then scraped her fingers down his chest, her nails gently pinching at his skin.

Scott's hands found their way to Gemma's breasts. He squeezed them, just how Gemma liked, massaging the flesh through the soft, smooth material of her bikini top.

Gemma reached forward and unzipped Scott's shorts. She pulled them open and tugged his boxers down a few inches, releasing his throbbing erection. She took his penis in her hand and began to stroke it, caressing the full length of his shaft.

Gemma pulled her head away from Scott's. "Go down on me," she insisted.

"You got it," said Scott, his maniacal smile growing ever wider. He then dropped to his knees. Now in prime position, he unbuttoned Gemma's denim shorts and slid them down to her ankles. Gemma willingly stepped out of them. Scott then kissed between her legs, pressing his lips firmly against her bikini bottoms.

Gemma closed her eyes, tipped her head back and sighed. She felt bad for Joe for around one second, before realising that she and Scott were still, technically, in a relationship. As such, she was doing nothing wrong. And besides, she had the same animalistic desires as every other human being on the face of the planet. She *needed* sex. If Joe wouldn't give it to her, then she would have to let Scott fuck her.

Scott pulled at the laces that tied the sides of Gemma's bikini, until the fabric fell loose and came away in his hand.

Gemma leaned back, placing her feet up onto the tree trunk, giving Scott an unobstructed view of her shaven snatch. Obediently, Scott began to lap at her vulva like a thirsty dog.

It felt *so* good. Scott's tongue flicked over her clitoris, then parted her labia, probing into her.

Gemma slid her fingers into Scott's hair, grinding her pelvis into his face, undeterred by the rough bark of the tree, that scraped painfully against her buttocks.

Soon, she climaxed.

Panting, she pulled Scott back up to his feet and kissed him, tasting her juices on her own tongue. Not that she minded; she always thought she tasted sweet, especially when mixed with their combined sweat.

She needed to feel him inside her. "Fuck me," she said, grabbing onto his stiff cock and guiding it towards her vagina.

Scott didn't need to be told twice. He pushed his hips forward, burying the entire length of his cock inside her. Gemma gasped, and then she squealed as Scott stroked in and out of her, the warmth inside growing and growing.

Scott slid his fingers into Gemma's bikini top, pushing the elasticated material aside, releasing her perfectly formed breasts. He moulded them, pinching her erect nipples between thumb and forefinger. It was painful, but that was exactly what Gemma liked. And then he bent, taking her right nipple in his mouth, his tongue drawing tight circles around the areola.

Another orgasm swelled. Gemma felt her vagina tighten, squeezing the life out of Scott penis. Seconds later, she felt him push in deep, as his balls tightened and unloaded his semen into her.

Gemma slumped back, arching her back over the thick trunk of the tree. The bark dug into her back, scraping her skin. But Gemma didn't care; she felt happy and satisfied.

Scott pulled his flaccid penis out of her. He reached up and ran his hand over Gemma's soft flesh, slick with sweat. "Fuck me, that was good," he said.

"Oh, yeah," moaned Gemma, the pleasure still coursing through her body. "Maybe we should forget about swimming. We could just stay here and spend the whole day fucking."

Scott laughed. "Sounds good to me."

Gemma groaned, her back aching as she sat upright. She pushed herself up and scooted herself forward, dropping back down to the ground. Scott's cum leaked out of her and trickled down her leg. She ignored this, and pulled her shorts back on, neglecting to reinstate her bikini bottoms. She then pulled her top back into place, so that the fabric once again covered her nipples. "Well," she said. "Either way, I gotta go take a piss."

Scott snorted. "I thought it was normally the man's job to say that."

"Well, do *you* need to piss?"

"No."

"There you go then. I do."

"You can just go here," said Scott, raising his eyebrows. "I don't mind. I'd quite like to watch."

Gemma tutted. "Don't be so *disgusting*." She stood on her tiptoes and planted a kiss on his cheek. As she did so, she took a hold of his penis and rubbed it gently. Immediately, she felt it begin to grow engorged. "I'll be right back. Don't go anywhere."

***

Scott watched as Gemma disappeared into the trees, leaving him standing there, his semi-hard cock hanging out of his shorts. As Gemma walked, her backside waggled, her buttocks swaying from side to side. That arse was perfect. Her tits were perfect. She was beautiful.

Scott hoped they might be together forever.

Scott crouched beside the rucksack. He flipped open the top and retrieved a bottle of beer from inside. He popped it open and guzzled the whole lot down. *Fucking was such thirsty work*, he thought to himself. He tossed the empty bottle aside, then pulled the blanket out of the bag.

Once the blanket was set out, Scott kicked off his shoes and his socks, dropped his shorts and kicked them aside too.

His dick was soft again now, so he tucked it back into his boxers.

He decided to leave his boxers on for now. The chances of anybody stumbling across them was highly unlikely, but just in case, he thought it best to *not* have his meat out on display.

He then laid back on the blanket and made himself comfortable, hands tucked up behind his head. He closed his eyes and relaxed. All around, birds were singing in the trees. The lightest of breezes floated through the branches overhead. Everything was so peaceful. Scott could've quite easily fallen asleep. Perhaps they could forget sex. Maybe he and Gemma could just cuddle and fall asleep in each other's arms.

But what was taking her so long? Perhaps he ought to go look for her.

Scott opened his eyes.

A dark shape towered over him, silhouetted against the sunlit sky. Was it an animal? It was big and brown, with beady black eyes. It was holding an axe.

Before Scott could say anything - before he could do anything - the shape had lifted the axe skyward and swung it down, sending the head of the axe crashing through his groin.

Scott's breath caught in his throat as his pelvis shattered into a million pieces. His left testicle ruptured, spilling its noodle-like contents and leaking from his lacerated scrotum. His penis was bisected, the spongy meat of the glans protruding from the ruined tube of flesh. His lap filled with blood, his boxer shorts saturated and clinging to his skin.

Scott looked down to his decimated crotch, the head of the axe buried deep into his body, the blade having sliced into his bladder and torn through his colon. He opened his mouth to scream.

But before he could make a sound, the assailant - that man, that beast - whatever the *fuck* it was - it raised its foot and slammed it downward, cracking Scott's nose bone and forcing it downward, into his face. Blood and mucus and frothy saliva burst forth and coated his face. Scott was choking, coughing. He could feel two teeth that had been knocked from his jaw filtering down past his tonsils and swimming down his throat.

With its foot on his face, the beast levered the axe out of his body. Immediately, his insides began to leak out.

The black shape lifted the axe one again.

***

Gemma unbuttoned her shorts and pulled them to her knees. She squatted, then loosened her bladder.

Once she was done, she turned back and walked the short distance to where she had left Scott waiting. She was feeling sexy and horny, and her body ached to feel Scott's warmth inside her once again.

"Hey there, Scotty-boy," said Gemma, as she knocked the trees aside. "Ready for round two?"

Then she froze.

Scott was dead. His head had been cleaved open, his skull cracked into a half-dozen pieces, his mashed brain leaking out into a puddle of blood, smeared in the dirt like a spilled jar of raspberry jam. Both eye sockets had broken outward, allowing the eyeballs to slide out, staring in opposite directions. His mandible jaw had been dismantled, snapped in two and torn from his face, splintered teeth here and there.

Gemma gasped. Her hands clamped over her mouth. Then she pulled them away and screamed at the top of her lungs, her throat immediately raw.

She turned to run.

But then the axe slammed into the side of her shoulder, tearing through the meat of her deltoid muscle, and fracturing her humerus.

She screamed again, the impact of the axe knocking her off her feet. Sobbing, she clamped her hands over the wound in her shoulder, the blood leaking through her fingers. There wasn't time to see who had attacked her; the axe was driving towards her once again.

Gemma raised her hands, her brain addled to the point that she believed doing so was a good idea. *It wasn't.* The blade of the axe slammed through her left hand, severing her thumb and two fingers, while snapping the other two fingers like twigs.

Terrified, her breaths coming rough and sporadic, Gemma rolled to her front. Weak, every ounce of energy suddenly sapped from her body, she tried to drag herself forward, the fingers of her good hand scraping through the mud, the fingers of her mangled hand as good as useless. It was futile; she was getting nowhere.

The agony she felt as the axe slammed into her back, splitting her scapular in half, and cracking at least five of her ribs, was the last thing that Gemma could remember.

After that, everything was black.

NINE

"Is this some sort of joke?" complained Bex, her head tipped back, her feet dragging behind her. "Surely we should be there by now."

Abbie could feel her frustration. They'd been walking for over two hours now. The best part of an hour had passed since they'd crossed the barbed wire fence.

"I've got to admit," Joe told Mike. "I think she's probably right. Where the fuck is this place?"

"I don't know," said Mike. "Scott said it was a few miles."

"Scott's full of shit!" snorted Bex. "There probably aren't any caves out here at all!"

Abbie laughed. "There's got to be *something* out here."

"Like what?"

"I don't know," said Abbie, shrugging her shoulders. She couldn't help but feel amused by Bex's annoyance.

"Alright," said Joe, stopping and turning to face the others, his arms stretched wide. "Do we want to go back, or what?"

"And waste all the time and effort we just spent walking out here?" moaned Bex.

"You're the one that's complaining!"

Bex shook her head. "Let's just keep walking," she sighed, as if it took all the effort in the world.

"Okay," said Abbie. "Half an hour. If we don't find anything in that time, we'll admit defeat and head back."

"Sounds like a plan to me," agreed Mike.

"Fine," said Bex. "Half an hour."

They found the house less than ten minutes later.

As they passed through the treeline and out of the woods, they found themselves in a wide-open expanse. In the middle of this clearing was the house. Then again, perhaps '*house*' wasn't the best descriptor for this particular building. It was more of a dilapidated shack, which looked as though it might fall down at any moment. It was, perhaps, no more than ten feet wide, by ten feet deep. The walls were constructed from planks of wood, hurriedly nailed together in a haphazard manner. There were no windows. A cracked, splintered sheet of plywood formed the door. The roof was made from corrugated tin sheets. A blue tarpaulin flapped from one side of the construction, presumably where part of the wall had fallen away.

"What the fuck is this?" said Joe, his face wrinkled in disgust.

"I have no idea," replied Mike. He and Joe then began to slowly approach the shack.

Both Abbie and Bex hung back a short distance, their backs to the trees. "Hold up," said Bex, waving her hands before her. "I don't like this. What if somebody *lives* in there?"

Joe stifled a laugh. "I don't think anybody lives in there, babe," he said. "Would *you* want to live in there?"

"There could be a bunch of homeless drug addicts living in there!"

"Well then, technically they wouldn't be homeless, would they?" Joe was grinning, finding himself to be hilarious. Clearly, Bex wasn't quite so amused. And Abbie seemed to find herself agreeing more so with Bex.

"What if this belongs to whoever put that sign up?" said Abbie, thinking back to the rusted barbed wire.

"I hope it does," said Joe, acting all macho. "Then I can ask them what the fuck they were thinking!"

Abbie and Bex looked at one another. It was clear to see that they were both thinking the same thing - this was a bad idea. But the boys were already nearing the shack, so it was already too late to stop them. So, both Abbie and Bex followed.

There were gaps in the walls of the shack, where the wood hadn't been lined up correctly. Some of the nails still jutted out, bent over where they had been clumsily hit with a hammer. The door hung off two corroded brass hinges. It was tied shut with a length of rope, one end tied around the handle, the other end tied to one of the bent nails that protruded from the frame.

Whoever had built this clearly didn't know what they were doing. It looked like a child had made it.

Mike tried to look through one of the gaps in the wall, using his hands to shade his eyes.

"You see anything?" asked Abbie.

Mike shook his head. "It's too dark in there."

Joe pulled at the rope that tied the door shut, unhooking it from the nail.

"What are you doing?" exclaimed Bex, as if she were shocked by this behaviour.

"I'm gonna take a look at what's in there," Joe said.

"You *can't* be serious."

"I don't think anybody lives here," Abbie said, reassuringly. She was looking at the building and wondering how anyone could *possibly* live there. She thought they were safe.

Apparently, Bex wasn't convinced. "How the fuck do you know?"

"Well - just look at it. Not much of a home, is it?"

"Come on," said Joe. "There's nothing to be scared of." He finished untying the door and allowed it to drop open.

Inside, thick dust hung in the air, the particles visible in the light that filtered in through the newly opened door. Joe stepped inside, knocking on the flimsy door as he went. "Knock knock," he said. "Anyone home?"

There was, of course, no reply.

Mike and Abbie followed Joe inside. Almost immediately the door slapped shut, hitting Bex in the back of the leg and causing her to spin in fright. Joe couldn't help but chuckle to himself. The air inside the shack reeked. It was musty and acrid and bitter, something like rotten meat. It reminded Abbie of a time - back when she was a teenager - when there had been an awful stink in her parent's kitchen. Her dad had had to pull all the panels from the cupboards and eventually found a dead rat behind the oven. It had tried to chew through one of the wires, but it had gotten electrocuted and died. And then it decomposed, filling the house with its vile smell.

But the stench in the shack was worse.

On one side of the structure, a dirty mattress laid on the floor, the fabric stained brown. It looked lumpy and uncomfortable; Abbie certainly didn't fancy spending the night.

"Well," said Joe, his eyes falling onto the disgusting mattress. "It looks like we found the local *'bone shack'*."

"What do you mean?" said Bex, holding her breath at the door, trying desperately to not breathe through her mouth.

"He means," said Abbie. "That this is where the kids come to lose their virginity."

"Oh. Nice. Well, I certainly wouldn't be having sex in here. It's fucking gross."

"I couldn't agree more."

"You sure?" asked Joe, beckoning for Bex to enter. "Maybe *we* could try it out." He placed his foot on the mattress and pushed, the springs groaning and creaking inside.

Bex pulled a face. "And roll around in other people's dried up bodily fluids? I'd rather go celibate."

Joe laughed. He turned to scan the shack. "What do we have here then?"

Abbie turned to follow his line of sight. He was looking at a dining table, the surface cluttered with broken plates and cracked glasses and rusted tin cans, the food inside having been only partly consumed. There were six chairs around the table. On each of the chairs sat a stuffed animal of some description. There was a brown bunny, with a red bowtie. There was a zebra, each of its stripes a different colour of the rainbow. There were two small bears, one grey and one white. The white one was missing both its eyes. There was what Abbie assumed was supposed to be an orange cat, but it was so deformed that it was impossible to tell. At the head of the table was a huge bear, at least five foot tall, its head and body plump and soft. It was so large that it had slumped forward, face down onto the table.

A sudden and distressing thought hit Abbie - it's a *teddy bear's picnic.*

Just like Scott's stupid story.

Joe picked up an empty can and sniffed it. Judging by the speed at which he dropped it, the smell couldn't have been all too pleasant.

"Be careful," said Bex. "This might be somebody's crack den. There's probably a bunch of dirty needles hidden about the place."

"What the fuck?" Mike muttered under his breath. Then, to the others, he said - "Take a look at this."

A picture calendar was hanging on the wall. It was four years out of date, and it was turned to the wrong month. But that wasn't what was so bizarre about it. Each page featured a picture of some nude girl, posing erotically, spreading her legs so the whole world could see her moist cunt. But then, on top of each picture, covering the woman's face, was the head of a teddy bear, the image roughly cut - or partly torn - from a catalogue.

"Well, that's really fucking weird," said Bex, venturing in through the door to get a closer look. "Who gets off on something like that?"

"Holy Jesus," said Mike. He was standing in the corner of the shack. Abbie moved closer, to see what he was looking at.

A pile of faeces lay in the corner of the room, compacted in and smeared up the walls. Numerous flies buzzed around it.

"*Fuuuuck me*," said Abbie. "No wonder it smells so bad in here. I think I'm gonna be sick."

Bex didn't bother to look. She was busy inspecting the plush animals seated around the table. "What's with all the bears?" she said. "Who put them here like this?"

"Who cares?" Replied Joe.

"I kinda do. Who built this place? And why have they put all these teddies here? It's fucking weird."

Abbie moved towards the large bear slumped at the head of the table. She crouched down for a better look. It was old, some of the fur having been worn away to bare fabric. That which remained was matted with filth. Parts of the material were torn, but somebody had tried to repair it, crude stitches woven through.

"What if it was Teddy?" said Abbie, knowing in her own mind that she sounded stupid. But that was all she could think of. *It was like some grotesque teddy bear's picnic.*

"The kid in Scott's story?" smirked Joe, clearly thinking that Abbie was joking. "The one that killed all those kids? You think *he* lives *here*? I doubt it somehow!"

"Well," said Abbie, reaching out for the big bear. "Whoever did this, it's really creepy."

As Abbie's fingers brushed against the bear, suddenly it moved. With a groan, it lifted its head.

Abbie screamed.

Bex screamed.

"Holy shit!" yelled Mike.

The bear grunted and groaned and writhed in its seat. Abbie noticed that the bear had been tied to the chair with nylon rope. But then she was being dragged out of the shack by Mike, and he was saying - "Go, go, go! Get the fuck out of here!"

And then the four of them were outside, running for their lives.

TEN

At the treeline, Abbie stopped. "Wait!" she called to the others, stopping them in their tracks.

"What is it?" panted Bex, her every breath short and rasping.

"Come on," urged Mike. "We've got to go!"

"No!" Abbie insisted. "We can't."

"What?" said Bex. "Why the fuck not?"

"That was a person back there!"

"Yeah, I know!" said Bex, her voice raised, the panic eating away at her. "It was a creepy fuckin' person, in a creepy fuckin' costume, sat at a creepy fuckin' table, in a creepy fuckin' house!"

"They could be hurt!" Abbie was starting to feel herself growing annoyed. Bex was being selfish. It was somewhat understandable - her brain had already engaged its '*fight or flight*' responses, and '*flight*' had long since won out. But there was somebody back there, and it looked to Abbie that they were in some serious trouble. "They need our help!"

"Help with what?"

Abbie couldn't quite understand it - was Bex stupid, or was she just confused? "Whoever that was," she said. "I've got a strange feeling that they didn't *want* to be there! They were *tied* to that chair!"

"So, let's phone the police and let them come and deal with it."

"Have you got signal on your phone? 'Cause I know I haven't."

Bex didn't respond. She put her hand on her hips and puffed out her cheeks, annoyed that Abbie would dare to be right.

Abbie continued - "How long is it gonna take us to hike back to the car and drive to somewhere we *can* get signal? Then how long is it gonna take the police to get here? We have to help that person. We can't leave them there."

Bex closed her eyes. "*FUCK!*" she bellowed, forcing every bit of air out of her lungs.

"Who would do that to somebody?" muttered Joe.

"I don't know," said Abbie, shaking her head. "But that doesn't matter right now, does it?"

"I guess not, no."

Abbie turned to Mike, silently pleading with him. "What do you think?"

Mike looked to Joe and Bex. Both looked terrified. But Abbie was terrified too. But any apprehension *she* felt, she forced to one side; saving the life of the person in that horrifying shack was far more important. Mike nodded. "Okay," he said. "Let's go."

Abbie and Mike headed back towards the shack. Joe placed his hand on Bex's shoulder. "Come on," he said, hoping to reassure her. "It's going to be okay."

Tears were streaming down Bex's face. "I don't want to go back in there," she cried.

"You don't have to. You can wait outside."

"By myself?"

"Yeah. But we'll be right inside. We're not gonna disappear. Come on."

Bex nodded and sighed. She and Joe then walked quickly, to catch up to Abbie and Mike.

Back at the shack, the door still hung wide open. Abbie peered in. The bear was still once again. It was seated upright now, although its head was lopped to one side. Slowly, she entered, Mike only one step behind.

At the door, Joe and Bex stopped. "You waiting here?" Joe asked Bex.

Bex shook her head. She grabbed onto Joe's arm and slowly they entered the shack.

As before, the door slapped shut, the thin plywood bending and creaking.

Abbie took cautious steps towards the table and the bear. The shack was practically silent, the quiet buzzing of the files even managing to mask her own breathing. She looked to the mattress and saw now that the material had split and that one of the springs was poking out through torn fabric. She hadn't before noticed just how dirty the floor was. Before, she hadn't cared, but now she took carefully considered steps, guiding her foot between the piles of litter, hoping to make as little noise as possible.

As Abbie and Mike neared, the bear lifted its head once again. "Urghhh…" it groaned, even that inhuman noise sounding laboured.

"Oh my God, oh my God, oh my God, oh my God…" repeated Bex, gripping onto Joe's arm even tighter now.

The bear wriggled in the chair, pulling against the restraints. Abbie could see now that the costume seemed to be homemade. Scraps of fur-lined fabric - presumably removed from other teddy bears - had been stitched together and reshaped into what it now was. The plastic eyes and nose had been glued onto the face, all off at strange angles, giving the bear a demented look.

Inside the costume - whoever that was in there - they were choking on their words, trying to speak.

"It's okay," said Abbie. "We're gonna get you out of here." She reached for the head of the costume.

"Be careful," said Mike, a heavy-looking feeling of dread etched into his pores.

Abbie nodded. She lifted the bear's head away, revealing the person inside. They had long, blonde hair, plastered with blood and stained crimson, draped across their face. Despite this, Abbie recognised her immediately. "Gemma?"

A dirty rag had been stuffed into Gemma's mouth and tied in place with a length of rope. Her nose was twisted off to one side, the skin split along the bridge, revealing the bone beneath. Both of her eyes were bruised black.

"Holy fuck," said Joe, pulling his arm away from Bex and crossing the shack in a single stride. He shoved past Abbie, then pulled the rope away from Gemma's face and tore the rag from her mouth. He then stroked her blood-soaked hair away from her face, tucking it delicately behind her ear. "What the fuck happened to you?"

Abbie was confused. The way Joe had reacted, the tender way in which he was showing concern for Gemma - it was almost as if he loved her.

Clearly, this fact hadn't escaped Bex either. "What the fuck is this?" she said, the initial terror she'd felt upon entering the shack now faded, replaced with pure heartbreak. "Joe? What's going on?"

Joe ignored Bex. He began to work at the ropes that bound Gemma to the chair. "Don't worry," he told her. "I'm going to get you out of here."

"He... He... He killed Scott," moaned Gemma, her voice weak, the words muddy as they spilled from her phlegm-filled throat. "He... Was... Going to kill me too."

Joe placed his hand on Gemma's cheek and stared into her eyes. "It's okay," he said. "You're safe now." His touch was delicate, like that of a man comforting a distressed lover.

"Hey!" screamed Bex, her voice shrill and venomous. She grabbed Joe by the shoulder. "I said *what the fuck is going on*? Are you fucking her?" Then, to Gemma, she asked - "Are you fucking *him*?"

Joe stood. He grabbed Bex by the shoulders. "This isn't the time or the place," he said, shaking his head.

"I think it's the perfect time, you prick!" said Bex, pulling away from his touch as if his fingers were burning her skin.

"No..." sobbed Gemma, tears streaming down her cheeks. "It's not. We... Uhh... We *have to* get out of here, right now. Before... Before *he* comes back."

"Before *who* comes back?" asked Abbie. She removed the ropes from Abbie's wrists and pulled away the fur. As soon as she did, part of her wished she hadn't. Gemma's left hand was destroyed, now no more than a mangled hunk of bloody flesh and bone hanging from the ruined stump. A savage gash shredded her right shoulder, the white of the bone visible through the muscle. She looked as though she should've been dead. "Can you stand?"

"I don't know." Abbie lifted Gemma's arm and looped it over her shoulder. Gemma's blood oozed from her wrecked hand and streaked down Abbie's t-shirt. But Abbie didn't care.

"No, wait," said Bex, a fury bubbling inside her. "I want to know what's been going on between these two." She aimed a finger directly at Joe's chest. "So, how long have you been bangin' her?"

Gemma moaned as Abbie helped her from the chair. Her breath caught in her lungs, her insides searing with agony. "That… That's not important right now."

"I wasn't talking to you, slut!" Bex spat through her teeth.

Abbie felt the gravity of the situation grinding down on her. Why was Bex being like this? Abbie didn't know for certain what was going on between Gemma and Joe, but that shouldn't have been the priority at that moment. Still, Bex seemed to be blind to the fact that Gemma had been attacked and violently disfigured. She didn't seem to understand what this *actually* meant.

It meant they were *all* in danger.

Joe snorted angrily, some guttural noise in the back of his throat. He turned back and hooked his shoulder under Gemma's other arm. "You know what?" he said. "Fuck this shit. If you want to stay here, you can. But I'm getting Gemma out of here."

Joe then helped Gemma towards the door, lifting her away from Abbie. As they went, Abbie was able to see the wound in Gemma's back, the flesh peeled away to reveal the shattered ribs below.

Joe pushed Bex aside. Bex gasped, undoubtedly shocked that Joe would dare to treat her that way. "No. Wait! I'm talkin' to you. You owe me a straight answer."

"Oh, go fuck yourself, Bex," said Joe. "I don't owe you shit."

Joe pulled open the door.

Gemma screamed, a sound so loud and shrill that it threatened to perforate Abbie's eardrums.

Standing in the doorway was a thing. A shape - big enough to fill the door and covered with brown hair.

No - not a shape. It was a teddy bear. Or, more specifically, a person dressed as a teddy bear.

It was six feet tall. Its fur, like that which had covered Gemma, was stitched together from shreds of other bears, like a patchwork made from the pelts of long deceased plushies. Its bulbous head was perfectly round, with two semi-circular ears sewed to the top. Its glassy, plastic eyes were black, like two shiny dots of coal. Although there was a short muzzle, there was no mouth or nose of which to speak.

The bear was holding an axe, the sharp edge of the head plastered with dried blood.

Gemma was still screaming - the sound seeming to grow louder and more deafening - until the bear raised the axe above its head and brought it down, dead-centre, into the top of her skull. Her head was bisected into two perfect halves, the two sides falling apart, her battered brain sloughing out and dropping to the filthy floor. The axe embedded into her neck. Gemma's limp carcass stumbled backward, crashing into the table and scattering the chairs, before dropping to the ground. As she fell, the axe was pulled from the bear's hands.

"*Run*!" screamed Mike, pushing Abbie and Bex out of the shack, knocking the bear to one side.

Abbie turned back. "Joe!" she yelled. "Come on! Let's go!" But Joe was now on his hands and knees, sobbing over Gemma's corpse.

A hand landed on Abbie's shoulder, causing her heart to twist inside her chest. But it was just Mike. "Abbie!" he said, dragging her towards the trees. "Now!"

Bex was already gone. Joe was still inside the shack. Gemma was dead. So was Scott, if what Gemma had said was true. But still, Mike had come back for *her*.

"Joe's still in there," said Abbie, looking back to the shack, the bear still standing in the doorway.

"Joe can look after himself," said Mike. "But *we* need to get out of here."

ELEVEN

Joe had tried to hold onto Gemma. He wished there was more he could've done. He'd have given his life for her if he could have. But he hadn't expected for some giant fucking teddy bear to be waiting for them outside, waiting to butcher them with a well-worn axe.

Who in their right mind *would have* expected such a thing?

As the axe had torn through Gemma's head, splattering Joe's face with her blood, he'd tried to support her, to hold her up. At that very moment, to *his* mind, she wasn't dead. She *couldn't* be dead. They had their whole lives ahead of them, their whole lives that they intended to spend together. They would have gotten married and bought a house and grown old together, Joe was sure of it. Gemma would've made an excellent mother. Joe had really wanted to see that.

Now, he wouldn't ever have the chance. As the axe was torn free from the hand of the bear, and as Gemma's brains had leaked from her shattered skull and squelched to the ground, Joe had tried to clamp her tight into his body. But the force of the blow had been too much and had knocked her loose from his arms.

She'd fallen clumsily and landed like a bag of loose bones.

The sight was horrific.

And then the others were gone. They left him behind. But he wasn't going to leave Gemma. She needed him. *He* needed *her*.

Joe could hear Abbie calling to him from outside the shack. Abbie was a good friend, both to him *and* Gemma. Her running, leaving them behind, was understandable; she was terrified, no doubt. He couldn't be mad at her for abandoning them.

But that was exactly what she *had* done. Joe wouldn't do the same to Gemma.

He dropped to his knees beside her corpse. He hadn't before noticed her dismantled hand, or the savage wound to her shoulder, or the mangled mound of flesh that hung from her back - *how had he missed any of those things?* Looking at them now, part of him imagined that perhaps Gemma's death was a blessing; she looked as though she'd been through hell - at least now she would suffer no more.

Joe rolled Gemma's corpse onto its back. Her face was an unrecognisable mess. Joe felt the tears begin to flow from his heavy eyes. "I'm sorry," he muttered, gently placing his hands on her chest. "I'm *so* sorry."

Movement behind him drew his attention.

The bear had entered the shack.

Joe didn't know what he should do. He didn't want to leave Gemma, but he understood now that there was nothing he could do for her. The only thing he could do was to try to survive. If he could get out of there, he could come back prepared. Then he could make this fucker pay for what he'd done.

He *had* to get out of there.

Joe stood, his shoulders heaving up and down, his deep breaths causing his lungs to ache. He considered fighting. He didn't know who was inside that bear costume, but, as far as he was concerned, there stood every chance he could take them. He could kill them, right there where they stood.

No. It wasn't worth the risk. If *he* died, then there would be nobody left to seek retribution for Gemma.

The bear stood motionless before him.

Joe gritted his teeth, lowered his head and charged forward, half expecting the bear to at least grab him, to try to stop him escaping.

But the bear didn't move. It just stood there, watching as Joe passed by, back out into the forest, his every breath cool and refreshing after those few short minutes breathing in the stagnant air of the shack.

Joe hated himself for leaving Gemma behind. He should have stayed. He should have fought. But instead, he was running. He should have...

SNAP!

The jaws of the bear trap sprung from the grass, clamping onto Joe's leg.

Joe felt his flesh tear and his bones snap. He screamed as he hit the ground, his ribs cracked and the air knocked from his lungs. The pain that tore through his nerves and exploded in his brain was like nothing he'd ever felt before.

Agony burning through every fibre, Joe rolled onto his back. He pushed himself up onto his elbows and looked down at his leg.

The jaws of the trap were constructed from steel, a quarter-inch thick. The blades were serrated; large teeth, filed to savage points, lined each of the jaws. An industrial spring - thick wire twisted into tight coils - clamped the metal against the organic matter of Joe's leg. There was blood everywhere. The skin had been peeled from his shin, exposing the tibia, itself cracked down the middle, the length split into two pieces. The meat of his calf muscle had been shredded and had slid down to his ankle, like a loose-fitting sock. From the knee down, his leg was little more than a bloody bone.

Joe wanted to scream again, but he couldn't. It was as if every ounce of energy had been drained from his body, and now he had nothing left to give.

He sat forward and tried to pull the trap open. If he could free himself, perhaps he could still make a run for it - not that his decimated leg would make it simple. The damage to his leg was irreparable, of that he was certain. If he ever made it to a hospital, he knew for a fact that they would amputate it. But that would never happen, if he couldn't escape the trap.

He pulled as hard as he could, but the jaws just wouldn't budge. As he pulled, the steel ground into the raw flesh and scraped across the splintered bone.

Joe moaned and dropped back down to the ground. He took a breath and sat back up.

The bear was coming for him. It had retrieved its axe, having torn it from Gemma's corpse.

It was at that moment that Joe gave up. There was nothing more he could do.

The bear swung the axe like a baseball bat. The head tore through the front of Joe's face, obliterating his upper jaw and tearing off half of his nose. A concoction of blood and mucus and saliva spurted from the wound, dragging a dozen loosened teeth with it.

The bear swung the axe again, back-hand this time. It slammed into Joe's temple, wedging its way through the bone, cracking open the top of his skull like a hard-boiled egg. His right eye popped, leaking orbital juices which flowed and mixed with the blood.

A blanket of darkness swamped Joe. His vision blurred and then dissipated to nothing. A numbness swept over his limbs.

The next blow landed on Joe's neck. His spinal column snapped. The cartilage of his larynx cracked and popped. His oesophagus collapsed in on itself. He began to choke on the air his lungs were desperately trying to draw in. With the next chop the blade embedded deeper, this time separating the vertebrae. The third cut removed the head entirely.

Joe was already dead when his severed head hit the ground.

***

Bex's feet pounded the forest floor. Her white pumps were stained black by the dirt.

Fuck it. There was a manic trying to kill her - the state of her sneakers was the least of her worries.

More concerning was the fact that she was now totally alone.

Bex had run, as fast as her legs could carry her. She pumped her arms and lifted her knees and pushed and pushed and pushed. But Abbie hadn't been behind her. Nor had Mike. They had both been there when they had left the shack. But, as far as Bex could tell, Abbie had gone back to try and help Joe.

Joe - that self-centred, egotistical bastard. He deserved whatever he had coming to him. Bex hoped he was dead. He and Gemma could spend an eternity together then, rotting in the bowels of hell.

No. That wasn't nice. Sure, right now she hated Joe and Gemma with equal measure. But perhaps this was all a misunderstanding. Perhaps they *weren't* sleeping with each other after all. At that moment, Bex realised she didn't actually *know* if Joe had been cheating. She couldn't be sure; not one hundred percent.

Not that it mattered anymore. Gemma was dead. There stood a good chance that Joe was dead too.

Exhausted, Bex stopped running. She bent, hands on knees, and breathed. And then, almost immediately, she straightened herself back up, realising that she was leaving herself prone, out there in the woods, all alone, with the bear somewhere behind her.

But she couldn't continue running. Her legs already seethed, the lactic acid building within the muscles. So, she began to walk, her eyes flitting all around, trying to stay alert to anyone - or any*thing* - that might be approaching.

"Abbie?" Bex whisper-shouted, not wanting to raise her voice too loudly, but also knowing that, if she remained too quiet, Abbie would never hear her. "Where are you?"

Nothing.

Bex continued onward. She hoped that she was heading in the direction of their camp. That was, to her mind, the best place to be right now. She expected that this was where Abbie and Mike would go too. She would head to the camp, then wait for the others. They could regroup, then get the fuck out of there.

"Abbie?"

A noise from somewhere behind. Bex turned to see the teddy bear, stalking through the trees towards her.

Bex felt her heart stop. Quickly, she darted behind a tree, pressing her back against the trunk and holding her breath, hoping and praying that this thing wouldn't find her.

What was she thinking? This wasn't a *thing*. It was a person - a man, most likely - dressed in a stupid fucking costume. Not that this thought made anything better; whoever it was, if they caught Bex, they'd kill her. Of that, there was no doubt.

Bex closed her eyes and listened. The bear was near; she could hear his feet crunching through the undergrowth. Bex could feel her heart pounding against her ribs, like an angry prisoner rattling the bars of his cell. She could hear it thudding in her head. And if *she* could hear it, did that mean the bear could hear it too?

Bex peered out from behind the tree. The bear was only a short distance away. He was looking around the forest, as if he didn't know which way he ought to go. *Good*. That meant he didn't know Bex was there.

Bex pulled her head back in behind the tree. There, she waited. Again, she heard the bear's footsteps. They were growing louder. He was getting closer. But then he passed by, continuing on, his back turned to Bex.

Sensing an opportunity, quickly, silently, she scooted around to the other side of the tree, keeping the thick trunk of the oak between herself and the bear-man. Again, she peered out. The bear was looking in her direction again. But how? She'd been so careful when she'd moved. She was sure she hadn't made a sound. Perhaps it was just a coincidence that he was now heading in her direction. No matter; Bex knew she had to do *something*.

There were two options; continue to hide, or make a run for it.

She made her decision quickly, hoping to keep as much distance as possible between herself and the bear. She pushed away from the tree and bolted.

Glancing over her shoulder, Bex saw the bear following. And so, she pushed harder, driving herself on through the forest, praying that she was heading in the right direction.

She ran for what felt like hours. Her joints - ankles, hips and knees - ached, her bones knocking together.

And then she hit the barbed wire.

The sharpened steel sliced into her thighs, biting into the fatty tissue. Bex tripped, her feet ripped from under her. As her body flipped, the barbs tore away strips of flesh, like a killer whale tearing through the flesh of a seal. She tried to steady herself, hands flailing. Her right arm tangled in the wire, and one of the barbs gouged a long gash along the length of her forearm. Blood squirted from her severed artery. And then she hit the ground.

Her head buzzing as if it were now home to a colony of bees, Bex tried to sit up. She was covered in blood, her skin slick and shiny, coated a deep red.

It was the fence, the one they'd crossed earlier. Did that mean she was heading in the right direction? Maybe. But maybe not. Bex didn't recognise this place. The '*keep out*' sign didn't appear to be there. It occurred to her that the barbed wire probably marked the entire circumference of the area that the teddy bear considered to be *his*. It was entirely likely that she'd run in completely the wrong direction. But it was also just as likely that the sign was just a short distance to her left, just beyond the trees.

Ignoring the searing pain on her legs, Bex stood. She turned to run…

And immediately slammed into the six-foot teddy bear.

Bex bounced from the bear's solid mass. She stumbled backward, into the barbed wire once again. The metal bit into her side, slicing into her love handles.

Bex screamed.

The bear reached out and grabbed her by the neck. Bex tried to fight, thrashing in his arms. But he was too big and strong. The bear wrestled Bex around, so that she was now facing away from him - facing towards the barbed wire.

Bex held her breath. The bear shoved her away, sending her face first into the wire. The force with which the bear had pushed her, had lifted her off her feet. As she fell, she did so directly into the wire. The barbs bit into her chin, scraped along her cheeks, tore through her nostrils, scratched against her eyeballs. It felt as though her entire face had been peeled away. She could taste her own blood, seeping into her mouth.

The bear stood over her. He took a handful of hair and yanked, pulling her off the ground.

Bex spit out a mouthful of blood. Face down, she saw that she was now hanging over the wire. And then she was being forced downwards, the wire biting into her throat, choking her. Bex tried to push on the wire, to force herself up, but it was no use; the bear was much too strong. The barbs pierced her skin, the steel strangling her.

But then the bear dragged her sideways, the pointed steel slashing open her throat.

Back and forth the bear ran Bex's throat along the wire, eventually lacerating her jugular. Blood gushed from the wound. Bex felt the life drain from her.

The bear continued running Bex's throat across the barbs. Soon enough, the wire had sawn halfway through Bex's neck.

The bear left the carcass there, suspended on the wire, her head barely hanging on, blood cascading from her like a waterfall.

***

It was the '*keep out*' sign. Abbie had never imagined she'd have been so happy to see it. But that meant that she and Mike were heading in the right direction.

Quickly, Mike jumped over the fence. He turned back and put a foot onto the top row of wire, forcing it down. He then held out his hands. "Let's go!" urged Mike.

Abbie took Mike's hands, placed her own foot onto the top wire and then pushed. Mike guided her over the fence, then pulled her into his body. "You okay?" he asked.

Abbie nodded.

But she wasn't okay. Gemma's head had been demolished. Joe was surely dead. Gemma had said that Scott was dead too. And now Bex was nowhere to be seen.

Was *she* dead too? Abbie really hoped not.

They had walked for almost an hour, from the camp to the barbed wire fence, so Abbie believed that, if they could keep a decent running pace, they would get back to camp in less than half that time. She just prayed that Bex had made it back there already, or that she was a lot closer than they were. She had been ahead of them, but then Abbie had lost sight of her in the trees. There was no telling in which direction she may have run.

When they arrived back at camp, it was clear that Bex had never made it back. "Shit!" screamed Abbie. "Where is she? Where's Bex?"

Mike shook his head, wordlessly confirming that, of course, he didn't know.

"Shit! Shit! Shit! She could be lost. Or... Or dead! What the fuck are we supposed to do now?"

"We *have to* get out of here," said Mike, solemnly. He looked like a sad puppy. He must've known how Abbie would respond; the look on his face begged her not to go on the offensive.

"We can't leave her out there," said Abbie, entirely focused on Bex now, Gemma and Joe and Scott having slipped her mind entirely. "Not with that psycho running around."

"No. You're right. Of course you're right. But we don't know where she is. She could be anywhere."

"We have to go back for her."

Mike's face scrunched itself into a ball. "That lunatic is out there, and you want to go back?" he scoffed. "Are you crazy?"

Abbie assumed that both of his qualifications were rhetorical. "You agreed. We can't leave her behind."

"I know. But we can't go back for her either. Not without putting our own lives at risk."

Abbie sighed, dejected, knowing that Mike was right. "Well," she said, her words coming slow. "Do you have any bright ideas?"

Mike shook his head. "No."

Abbie paused for a moment, thinking. She had to help Bex. They couldn't leave without her. That just wouldn't be right. It wouldn't be *fair*. "Well, I don't either. So, I'm going back, even if I have to go alone."

Abbie turned away from Mike. She began to walk back towards the trees, from where she had just come. She'd walk all the way back to the shack if she had to. If she found Bex dead, she'd be heart broken. But at least that way, she'd know.

"Wait!" called Mike, jogging to catch up to Abbie. "Don't be so stupid. You don't have to go alone."

Abbie turned to face him, a deep sense of relief flooding out of her. "Good," she said, tears falling from her eyes all of a sudden. "I really don't want to do this alone."

"You don't have to," said Mike, placing his hands onto her shoulders. "I'm here for you. I'm *always* her for you."

And then they kissed. Mike's lips were soft, but his stubble was rough, and it pricked at Abbie's skin. But she didn't care. This just felt so right. Mike truly did care for her; she could see that now. A soft warmth expanded in her heart. And then she knew - everything was going to be alright.

When she pulled away, she could feel herself smiling.

But then her heart sank.

The blade of the axe slammed vertically into Mike's right shoulder, snapping his collarbone like a twig. Blood splattered Abbie's face as Mike grunted, his face distorted into something so incredibly ugly. He looked like death.

The teddy bear had come out of nowhere. Abbie couldn't help but feel that this was her fault; she'd been distracted. If she'd been focused on the task at hand, perhaps she'd have seen him coming. As it was, she hadn't. And now he was killing Mike.

The bear kicked Mike in the back, tearing the axe out of his arm, and sending him crashing through one of the tents.

Abbie turned. She ran. She didn't get far.

Almost instantly, her foot caught on the guy line of one of the tents. Her ankle twisted back and she hit the ground hard, grazing her chin. Quickly, she flipped over. The bear towered over her. It held the axe above its head.

Abbie cowered away, feeling ashamed of herself.

The bear brought the axe down, slamming the base of the wooden handle into the side of Abbie's head.

Black.

TWELVE

When Abbie awoke, she was drenched in sweat. Her vision was black and she could barely breathe. It felt as though her lungs were filled with cotton wool. A horrible stench filtered up her nose, stinging her eyes. It smelled like ammonia, mixed with rotten eggs. Abbie thought she might vomit. Her stomach twisted and churned, but nothing came up.

There was something over Abbie's head. That was why she couldn't see. That was why she couldn't breathe. Tiny pinpricks of light flickered in her peripheral. Abbie realised then that she was looking *through* some sort of fabric.

She could taste something sour in her mouth, and her jaw was locked. It was a gag; she was sure of it. If it were anything like the one that had been stuffed into Gemma's mouth earlier, it would be no more than a dirty rag, tied in place with a rope.

And there were ropes tied around her wrists, binding them to something hard at her side. Abbie tried to pull her arms away, but the ropes burned into her skin.

And then, more light filtered in, as something moved beyond her vision. There was a sound, creaking wood. Abbie could sense somebody standing close to her. The hairs on her arms stood on end.

And then whatever it was that had been covering her head was lifted away.

She was back in the shack. She was seated before the table, tied to the chair, just as Gemma had been earlier. As her eyes focused, Abbie saw that she was surrounded by teddies, all sitting politely at the table, just as they had been before. But now, sat at the other end of the table was a face Abbie recognised.

Mike was bound and gagged, exactly as she was.

And then Abbie turned her attention to the thing standing beside her.

The teddy bear.

It loomed over Abbie, holding by its side the head of another teddy. It was that, Abbie realised, that had been removed from her head. She looked over her body to see that she was now dressed in the furry costume that Gemma had previously been dressed in.

Suddenly, something dawned on Abbie; she was a replacement for Gemma.

The bear tossed the head aside, allowing it to clatter into the rest of the junk that littered the floor, before rolling onto the dirty mattress. It then moved in close to Abbie and held her by the chin, tipping her head back, so that they could be face to face.

Abbie squeezed her eyes tight shut. She could hear the bear breathing, heavy and raspy, as if its lungs were full of fluid. And it stank of piss and shit, as if it hadn't bathed in years. The bear tilted its head and looked her over, shifting her chin from one side to the next. And then, apparently satisfied, it released her and turned away. It crouched before a steel toolbox, flung open the lid and began to rummage through the contents.

Abbie took a breath. Slowly, she opened her eyes.

Looking over the table, she saw that before each of the stuffed animals was a plate. Covering each plate was an upturned bowl - some plastic, some ceramic. One of the bowls was glass mixing bowl, the inside plastered with something dark red.

Mike groaned as he began to come around.

Abbie twisted her head, rotating it, straining her neck, until the gag worked its way loose. "Mike?" she croaked, her voice raw.

The bear's head snapped around sharply. Its stony black eyes stared at her, despite the fact that it couldn't possibly be seeing her. Not through *those* eyes, anyway.

Still, Abbie froze. Mike groaned again, his head slumping forward. The bear looked from Abbie to Mike, then back to Abbie. It stood and once again moved in close. It looked Abbie over, inspecting her face. It was as if it knew something was amiss, it just couldn't place what it was.

The bear straightened up.

"What do you want from us," moaned Abbie. "Please. You can't do this. You have to let us go."

The bear ignored her. It turned to face Mike. From the table, it took a long butcher's knife. The blade was rusted and blunt, but there was no doubt in Abbie's mind that it could still do some serious damage.

"No," said Abbie. "Wait."

The bear ignored her. It moved in closer to Mike.

Abbie panicked.

"TEDDY!" she yelled. At first, she was unsure of why she had done so, but then her brain raced to catch up and she understood fully. This bear - or, more precisely, the man standing before her, *dressed* as a bear - this *was* Teddy, the boy from Scott's stupid story.

Edward Tedstone, the bullied boy who killed all those kids and cut them up into tiny pieces. The story was true. And this was his home now. He must've been living there since the murders. He must've run away, and, desperate to never return home and face the consequences of what he'd done, he'd built himself a house in the middle of the woods.

He was just defending his property, thought Abbie.

Slowly, Teddy turned to face Abbie, clearly recognising his name.

"That's right, isn't it?" Abbie continued, thinking that if she let him know that *she* knew who he was, she might somehow be able to reason with him. "Your name is Teddy. You were bullied by some horrible boys, just because you were different. But you got them back, didn't you? You made them pay. But we're not those bullies. We're good people. You don't have to do this. You could just let us go."

Teddy didn't respond.

Abbie thought for a moment, then continued - "What do you say? We can go, and never come back. We won't tell anybody about you, or about what you did. You can carry on living out here. This is your home. But we didn't know that. We didn't mean to break in here. We're very, very sorry for that. So? How about it?"

Teddy remained silent. It occurred to Abbie that maybe he couldn't talk, even if he'd wanted to. If he'd lived out here, having spent his entire life all alone, he'd never have had anybody to speak to. Perhaps he never learned *how* to talk.

But then Teddy planted the knife into the table, embedding the blade into the wood. It remained vertical, vibrating back and forth, even after he'd released his grip.

Quickly, Teddy approached Abbie, picking up the plate that had sat on the table before her. He held it up in front of her face, then slowly removed the overturned bowl.

Abbie gasped.

On the plate was a severed hand. Gashes ran along the back, the flesh separated into vast chasms, the bones visible beneath. Blood stained every inch of the lacerated skin. The plate itself was garnished with twigs and dead insects.

Abbie's breath stuttered. "Oh my God…" she moaned. "Oh God, oh God, oh God…"

Teddy laughed, a scratchy, scraping noise from deep in his throat. It was then that Abbie noticed that a rough hole had been cut into the base of the bear's head. Through it, she could see the man's mouth. His smile was full of crooked, rotten teeth, the gaps between them making them look almost inhuman.

"What the fuck is this?" sobbed Abbie, tears streaking down her cheeks.

Teddy returned the plate to the table. He then moved down the table, lifting the covers from the other plates. One contained a heart and a kidney, and what Abbie believed to be part of a liver, all swimming in a puddle of blood. Another held a coil of intestines, which, once the cover was removed, snaked and slopped from the plate. Another was full to the brim with disembodied eyeballs. In the middle of another plate sat a severed penis, cut away at the root, the edge of the plate decorated with severed fingers and ears.

Abbie's face felt numb. If she could've seen herself in a mirror, she'd have seen that her face had turned grey, every drop of colour having leaked from her cheeks.

Mike groaned again, his head flopping from one shoulder to the other.

"Mike!" said Abbie, hoping that, if he were to wake up, he might know what to do. "Mike! Mike!"

Teddy laughed again. He sounded gleeful, like he was gaining a great deal of pleasure from watching Abbie squirm.

"Mike! Mike!"

Mike didn't wake. He just groaned once again.

"Please," begged Abbie, crying harder now. "You have to let us go. You're fucking *insane*! You *have* to let us go!"

Still snorting some kind of vile laughter, Teddy moved behind Mike. He put his hands on the back of Mike's chair and tipped it back. Then, with the chair now on two legs, Teddy dragged it across the shack and dropped it in front of Abbie, positioning Mike's unconscious self so that he was facing Abbie.

"Mike!" said Abbie, her words shrill now. "Please wake up! You *have* to wake up! We need to get out of here. Mike!"

Teddy untied Mike's gag and pulled the rag from his mouth. Mike woke then, his lungs suddenly filling with clean air. "Wha… What's going on?" he mumbled.

"Mike?"

Mike lifted his head. He blinked rapidly, clearing the clouds from his vision. "Abbie? What the fuck is going on?" He looked around the shack, the facts of the predicament in which he had found himself slowly sinking in. He looked to the table, where the dismembered body parts still sat in pools of blood. "Oh…" he said, swallowing his own words in order to stifle the torrents of puke threatening to rise in his gullet.

"Mike," said Abbie, crying harder still. "What are we supposed to do? How do we get out of this mess?"

Mike shook his head. "I… I…" And then he saw Teddy from the corner of his eye, and he froze.

"Mike," said Abbie sniffing back her tears, trying to remain calm. "It's Teddy, the boy from Scott's story. He lives here."

"What the fuck," spluttered Mike, coughing up balls of spit, saliva trailing down his chin. "Teddy? This is fucking insane. Is this some sort of joke? 'Cause if it is, it isn't funny. Untie us now! Let us go! Let us fuckin' go!"

Teddy pounced. He grabbed Mike by the chin and yanked his head back. Mike writhed in the chair, but found he was fighting a losing battle against the ropes that bound his wrists. He groaned. Then he screamed.

"Let go of him!" bellowed Abbie. "Please, don't!"

Teddy was holding a spoon.

"Don't do this," sobbed Abbie. "Please…"

Teddy plunged the spoon into Mike's eye. Despite how blunt the spoon was, the stainless steel sliced through the delicate skin of Mike's eyelid with ease. It then slid into the socket, between the eyeball and the wall of the orbital.

Mike screamed as blood squirted from his face. The sticky, red liquid poured down his cheek and dripped from his chin.

"No!" Abbie screamed.

Mike was wailing, gargling his own saliva. Teddy wiggled the spoon around in his eye socket, running it three-hundred and sixty degrees around his eyeball, tearing through the soft, delicate flesh. And then, levering the handle of the spoon against Mike's cheek, he popped the eyeball from the socket.

Abbie's heart felt like a block of ice. She felt as though she had to force it to beat. Mike was a good man; he didn't deserve this. But there was nothing she could do to help him. She could only watch as Teddy dismantled his face.

The eyeball slipped off the spoon and hung from the stem, splattering against Mike's chin. Teddy dug his fingers into the now empty eye socket, looped the ocular nerve around his dirty fingers and pulled. The meat cracked and squelched as it gave way. Exhausted - and looking as though he were half dead - Mike slumped back in the chair. Teddy placed the eyeball back onto the spoon, carefully balancing it, like a child running an egg-and-spoon race. He then looked to Abbie.

All of sudden, it hit Abbie like a blow from a sledgehammer. She knew exactly what Teddy wanted her to do.

Teddy pushed the spoon in towards her face. Abbie felt the cool stainless touching her lips. She tasted iron in her mouth; Mike's blood seeping in. She bit her teeth down as hard as she could, clamping her lips together. And then Teddy's hand was on her chin, squeezing her jaw. The pain was excruciating. She thought he might squeeze so hard that her mandible snapped in two. And then there was nothing more she could do - her mouth fell open.

Teddy stuffed the spoon into her mouth, tipped it up and pulled it out, leaving the eyeball behind.

Disgusted, Abbie immediately spat the eyeball out.

Clearly agitated, Teddy scooped the eyeball up from the floor then forced it back into Abbie's mouth, pressing his palm into her face so she couldn't spit it out again. Then, to make the gravity of the situation even clearer, he pulled the rusty knife from out of the table and held it to Mike's throat.

Teddy hadn't spoken with words, but the implication was clear; if Abbie didn't do as he wanted, he'd cut Mike's neck wide open.

And so, Abbie did as she thought Teddy wanted; she used her tongue to swill the eyeball around her mouth, moved it into position between her rear molars, then bit down. The eyeball burst, filling her mouth with some disgusting, foul-tasting liquid. She could feel it oozing over her lips. And then she began to chew, crunching through the hard material of the lens and the cornea, trying her best to slice through it with her incisors. She chewed and chewed and chewed, until the eye was no more than a masticated lump of sclera. Then she swallowed it down.

Laughing once again, Teddy stepped away, removing the knife from Mike's neck.

Abbie coughed and spluttered, what little remained of Mike's eyeball seeping out of her mouth and drooling down her chin. A sense of relief bubbled in her chest, thankful that Mike was still alive.

But that was short-lived.

Teddy slammed the blade into Mike's stomach.

Mike screamed.

Abbie cried.

Teddy drew the knife sideways, the dull blade ripping and tearing at the meaty flesh of Mike's belly. Blood poured from the wound, coating his legs, pouring from his lap, splashing into a fresh puddle on the ground beneath him. Once Mike's stomach was opened, Teddy embedded the knife into the table once again. He then reached inside of Mike and began to drag his entrails out.

And Mike was still alive. Abbie couldn't believe her eyes. He was grunting and twisting, pulling at his restraints, while Teddy continued to eviscerate him.

When Teddy had removed enough of Mike's intestinal tract, he then began to feed it to him, stuffing it into his mouth, forcing Mike to eat himself. Delirious with pain, Mike gladly obliged, chomping on his own guts until he finally fell dead.

Abbie tried to scream, but what came was little more than a whimper.

Again, Teddy laughed, that abhorrent choking sound, scraping away at his vocal cords. He moved behind Mike once again, tipped his chair back and dragged him across the shack, his intestines dragging along the floor. Teddy dragged Mike's corpse out through the door.

Alone now, Abbie closed her eyes and tried to summon the strength to survive.

The problem was, she wasn't sure that she had that strength within her.

THIRTEEN

When Teddy finally came back, Abbie had her eyes closed. She was exhausted. She had spent the time that Teddy was gone, trying to free herself from the chair. She had pulled and twisted and wriggled, trying to loosen the ropes that bound her wrists to the wooden arms of the chair. But, other than having the abrasive hemp scrape away at her epidermis, she didn't feel like she'd achieved much.

As the door slammed open, Teddy lurching clumsily into the shack, Abbie closed her eyes, hoping - *praying* - that he might just leave her be.

Almost immediately, she realised that this was not going to be the case.

Teddy hit her, ramming the heel of his open palm into her jaw. Abbie's head snapped back and she gasped, furious with herself for having given up the game so easily. "Please," she begged once again, despite her certainty that this would have little-to-no effect on Teddy. "Don't do this. Please, let me go."

Nothing.

Teddy was holding a glass pitcher. It was full to the brim with some dark liquid. In the dull light that broke in through the cracks in the walls, it looked black. But, considering the mountain of dismembered body parts strewn across the table, she already knew that this was blood. He set the pitcher down.

There were a number of plastic cups and glass tumblers on the table. Teddy picked up the two nearest to him; both were short glasses, coated in dust and grime. He placed one before Abbie, while holding onto the other. He then picked up the pitcher of blood and filled both glasses. He set the pitcher down once again, then picked up Abbie's glass.

Teddy clinked the two glasses together. A wet, guttural sound rolled out of his throat. Was he trying to speak? If so, the word was unintelligible. But then Abbie realised what he was trying to say.

He was trying to say *"Cheers!"*.

Teddy tipped his head back and swallowed down the blood in one gulp. He then pushed in close to Abbie, offering the filled glass up to her mouth.

Abbie twisted her head away, puckering her lips so that nothing might pass them. But Teddy was relentless. He continued pushing the glass against her lips, until Abbie felt her teeth biting into her flesh. She couldn't help it then - she opened her mouth. Teddy tipped the glass, filling Abbie's mouth with blood. It choked her, gagged her, flowed over her lips and cheeks, pouring onto her chest, making the inside of the bear costume sticky against her skin.

She coughed, spitting out as much of the blood as she could. Then she puked, the wave of vomit forcing itself up her throat and spilling into her lap.

Teddy was laughing again. He pulled up a chair and took a seat at the opposite end of the table, directly facing Abbie. He pulled a plate towards himself, one that contained a human tongue. He then picked up a knife and fork and began to carve the meat.

Abbie felt disgusting. The coppery taste of blood still lingered in her mouth, combined with the acidic tang of bile. But what could she do? Was this all there was for her now? Would she spend the rest of her days being tormented by a man - dressed as a giant teddy bear - being forced to eat human flesh, until the bear grew bored and slaughtered her too? "Oh God," Abbie moaned. "Please don't kill me. Just let me go."

Teddy lifted the fork. A sliver of raw meat flapped from the prongs, dripping with blood. He pushed it through the ragged bear's mouth, and into the human mouth beneath. He chewed noisily, saliva and blood slapping between his jaws.

"Oh my God! Oh my God!" screamed Abbie. A fury was building inside her. *How dare he do this to her*! She pulled at her restraints once again and she was sure she felt them loosen. "This is fucking insane! Let me go, you fucking monster!"

Teddy laughed. He took another slice of tongue meat and fed it into his mouth.

"You're crazy! It's no wonder the other kids picked on you! What kind of a boy plays with teddy bears? You had no real friends, is that it? Well, these bears aren't real, you know? Nobody liked you cause you're fucking insane!"

Teddy paused. He stopped chewing. He lowered his knife and fork. Although Abbie couldn't see his real eyes, she could sense him staring at her.

And then he burst out in laughter and continued to eat.

Abbie wriggled her hands. She felt the rope tied around her right wrist slip over the bone, down to her thumb.

"What's so funny?" Abbie continued. "The fact that you're crazy? Or the fact that you're a grown man who still likes to play with stuffed animals?"

Teddy continued to laugh.

"Huh? Which is it, you fuckin' psychopathic loser?"

Angrily, Teddy slammed his fists down on the table causing the plates to rattle and their grotesque contents to spill. Terrified, Abbie's heart shrivelled like a raisin. Suddenly, she regretted provoking him. But then Teddy howled, snorting and scoffing the most hideous laugh Abbie had ever heard.

Abbie's blood began to boil. Her head throbbed, her brain ached. "What the fuck are you laughing at? *This isn't funny*! This isn't a fuckin' joke! You aren't normal. You're crazy!"

Teddy placed the last of the tongue in his mouth, chewed it, then swallowed.

"You fucking bastard! Let me go!"

Teddy was laughing.

Abbie's head felt as though it were expanding, inflating like a balloon, ready to go pop. She felt dizzy. Lights flickered, burning her retinas.

Still, Teddy was laughing.

"You're crazy!" screamed Abbie, her voice growing horse. "You're crazy! You're crazy! YOU'RE CRAZY!"

Then…

Abbie couldn't believe her eyes.

The stuffed animals sitting at the table began to laugh in unison with Teddy. Their little mouths flapped open and closed, their heads rolling on their shoulders. Their voices were high-pitched, crackling in their tiny, inhuman throats. Their soft, fluffy hands banged the table excitedly. Teddy laughed harder. When he did so, the little bears laughed harder too.

Abbie had finally cracked. She'd gone mad. Maybe it wasn't Teddy who was insane; maybe it was Abbie herself.

The little animals continued to laugh as Teddy stood from the table. He approached Abbie and, using a severed hand he picked up from the table, he stroked her hair back, away from her sweaty forehead. Abbie gasped and writhed, pulling away from the morbid touch of the cold, dead, grey-skinned hand. She pulled at her arms, ignoring the pain of the rope chewing through her wrists.

The bears kept laughing.

Teddy lifted the severed hand to his mouth, sucking in a finger, licking along the length of the appendage. He then bit in, peeling away a strip of meat from the knuckle to the fingertip.

Still the bears were laughing.

Abbie pulled her right hand free. Quickly, she darted forward and snatched up the rusty knife. Then, just as quickly, she lifted it above her head and slammed it downward, through the back of Teddy's hand, embedding it into the table. She heard at least one of his metacarpal bones snap.

Teddy bellowed in agony, as blood squirted from the wound, coating the thick fur of his gloved hand crimson. Immediately, those little bears stopped laughing and fell still once again.

But Abbie didn't care about that. She was too busy untying the rope around her left wrist to even notice. And then she was free. She ran, crashing out of the shack and into the forest, leaving Teddy pinned to the blood-soaked dining table.

Every breath was painful, her diaphragm burning as it tried desperately to suck the air into her lungs. But Abbie forced her brain to shove this to one side. She couldn't allow her mind to wonder. She had to stay focused. If she even dared to look back, that would almost certainly result in her death.

Teddy was behind her; she was sure of it. She could sense him closing in.

The branches of the trees whipped against Abbie's bare arms and legs, stinging her over and over, like a swarm of angry bees. But she kept going, ignoring the pain. She knew that if she wanted to survive, that was exactly what she needed to do.

She could hear Teddy chasing her. She could hear his feet scraping through the dirt. Despite telling herself that she shouldn't - despite telling herself that it was a waste of precious nanoseconds - Abbie looked back over her shoulder.

Sure enough, Teddy was there. He was carrying the rusty knife that had, just moments ago, been impaled through his hand. Blood coated the blade and dripped from the point.

Abbie continued on, pushing through the forest.

It felt as though she had been running for an eternity. Her muscles were beginning to seize. Her body seemed to be growing heavier, her legs screaming out as they struggled to convey her forward. But then Abbie noticed that the noise behind her had stopped. She looked back.

Teddy was no longer there.

Abbie's heels skidded through the dirt as she slammed on the brakes, almost sending herself crashing to the floor. On shaky legs, she spun three-sixty, desperately searching for Teddy.

She found him. He was, perhaps, thirty meters away, off to her right. He was standing, shoulders heaving as if he himself could hardly breath, his head flicking from side to side, no doubt searching for Abbie, as she had been searching for him. He must've lost track of her through the trees.

This is my chance, thought Abbie. He didn't know where she was. She could hide. If she could get to someplace where he couldn't find her, she could hunker down and wait out the night. He'd give up his search eventually. When he did, then she could make her move.

But none of that mattered. Teddy's beady black eyes fell upon her. And then he was running in her direction.

Fuck.

Abbie turned and ran. One step, two steps, three steps - then the forest floor disappeared from under her feet and she was tumbling down a steep slope, her arms and her back banging painfully against the ground, her legs freewheeling. She hit the bottom with a thud, the wind knocked from her sails. "Ughhh…" she groaned, as she heaved herself up to her hands and knees.

Teddy stood at the top of the hill, looking down.

Abbie groaned. She pushed herself up to her feet and ran once again.

Behind her, Teddy scooted down the bank, moving from one tree to the next, using them for support.

Abbie ran and ran and ran, as if her life depended on it. Of course, her life *did* depend on it. There was no way she was going to let this fucker kill her, not now, not after everything she'd been through.

Her foot caught on a tree root, twisting her ankle back to position that it really shouldn't have been able to reach. Abbie squealed as she fell, eating the dirt.

That was it. She was done for.

Teddy was right there. Abbie rolled to her back just in time to see Teddy pouncing, knife raised. She lifted her knee and aimed for his groin. Direct hit. Teddy crumpled, moaning as he rolled away, his hands clamped between his legs.

Abbie flipped to her front. Like a mouse trying to escape the clutches of a hungry cat, she scratched and scraped at the forest floor, until she was back to her feet.

But then she was down again, Teddy's hand wrapped around her ankle, dragging her back in towards himself. "No!" screamed Abbie. "Let go of me!"

Abbie squirmed in Teddy's grip. When Teddy lifted his knife and drove it down towards her face, she only just managed to avoid it. She failed to avoid his second attempt, however. This time, he aimed lower. The blade penetrated Abbie's shoulder, tearing the ligaments that held her collarbone in place.

Abbie cried.

Teddy pulled the knife free. He then pulled himself on top of Abbie, straddling her waist. With both hands on the hilt of the knife, he raised it above his head.

Abbie's hands scrabbled through the dirt. Her fingertips brushed against something hard. A rock. She grabbed it and swung with all her might, ploughing it into the side of Teddy's head.

Dazed, Teddy tumbled off of Abbie.

With adrenaline speeding through her body, Abbie practically jumped to her feet. She pounced onto Teddy and hit him with the rock once again. Teddy's body jerked beneath her, as the blow cracked his skull.

Abbie then sat her full weight onto Teddy's chest and began to slam the rock into his face, over and over again.

One.

Two.

Three.

Four.

Five.

With every blow, Abbie felt Teddy's skull give way a little more. Every impact was accompanied by the crunching of bone and the squelch of tearing flesh.

Abbie continued to hit Teddy. She must've hit him a thousand times. Through the gaping mouth of the bears head, she saw his human mouth hanging wide, twisted off to one side, as the bone that should've been there to support it had been entirely destroyed. Blood seeped over his lips and soaked into the soft fabric of the costume.

Teddy was dead. He wasn't struggling. He wasn't moving *at all*. Abbie could feel his chest beneath her, entirely still, not breathing.

Abbie dropped the rock. She sat still momentarily, while she caught her breath. And then she began to cry.

Get a grip, Abbie told herself. Her nightmare may have been over, but she still needed to get out of there. She stood, her legs like jelly, and walked away.

Her brain swam in a river of nothingness. It was as if she had been enveloped by thick, black clouds. It was if she no longer inhabited her own body. She felt as though she were no longer in control. She walked in one direction or another. Where she was headed, she had no clue.

But she was alive. That was the main thing.

Abbie collapsed, her legs crumbling, face first into the dirt.

FOURTEEN

"Please," said the police officer, her soothing voice calm and kind. "Tell me again - what exactly happened?"

"I just told you," said Abbie, her body aching all over. Her joints throbbed, happy to have finally been given some respite. The doctors had stitched her up and filled her full of painkillers. "I told the other officer twice, too!"

"Please. Tell *me* again. This will be the last time, I promise." The police officer was smiling. Her brunette hair was tied back into a neat bun and she smelled like soap.

When Abbie had awoken, she'd found herself lying in a hospital bed. Everything around her was white and clean. Everything smelled as fresh as the officer now sitting before her. It was nothing like that filthy shack, the walls stained with blood and shit, littered with rotting, human body parts.

The police had been *waiting* for her to wake. Apparently, they'd had an officer posted outside the door to her room, ever since the very moment she'd arrived. Once the doctors had checked her over, the police had begun to interrogate her. Abbie tried her best to explain everything. She told them *every* detail. She told them all about Teddy and his vile house of horrors, hidden in the woods. She told them how he'd murdered her friends and then cut them up and feasted on their flesh. She told them how she'd escaped and how she'd cracked Teddy's head open with a rock, and then beaten him to a bloody pulp. The only thing she neglected to tell them about was the collection of stuffed animals that had come to life and laughed at her; she couldn't be *sure* that that had actually happened. If she told them about that, they'd almost certainly think she was crazy.

Crazier than they *already* thought she was.

Abbie sighed, slinking down deeper into the comfortable mattress that now caressed her entire body. "Where should I begin?"

The officer flipped open her notepad and began to quickly scan through the notes she'd made the last time Abbie had told her story. "So," said the officer. "There were six of you altogether, right? You and your five friends? And now, to the best of your knowledge, they are all dead?"

Abbie nodded. "Teddy killed them."

"Right - a man dressed in a giant teddy bear costume. And you believe you knew who this man was?"

Abbie nodded again. "Teddy. The boy who killed those bullies. Out in the woods. It was a long time ago."

The officer nodded this time. "I've heard this story before. We all have. If you live around these parts, you can't *help* but hear about poor old Teddy. But I assure you - *that* never happened."

The first police officer - the big, burly man, with a fat belly and a scruffy beard - had told her the same thing. Teddy - the boy - didn't exist. But Abbie *knew* that he did. Who else could that have been, running around in the woods, dressed the way he was, killing and eating people? That *had* to be Teddy.

The officer continued - "That story is no more than a local *urban legend*. The kids tell that story just to try and scare each other."

Abbie shook her head now. "No," she said. "He exists. He killed my friends."

"Listen - Abbie," said the officer, softening the tone of her voice to an almost patronising level. She sat forward in her chair. "I believe you. Your friends *are* missing. But were they killed by a boy from a spooky story? I honestly doubt it."

An old man had found her while out walking his dog. She had been battered and bloody (no shit). It was he who had called the police, who arranged for her to be rescued from the woods and taken to the hospital. She owed him her life. But, although they had found *her*, they hadn't found anybody else. There was no sign of Bex. No sign of Mike or Joe. No sign of Gemma or Scott. They *hadn't* found Teddy's corpse, his head reduced to a stain on the ground where she had left him. They *didn't* find the run-down, beaten-up shack, filled with human remains.

They found… *absolutely nothing.*

"There's no doubt in my mind," said the police officer. "That you and your friends were attacked. Your wounds, most certainly, are not self-inflicted. *Something* happened to them. Was it the boy? No, I don't think so." She sat back in her chair. "Anyway, tell me about how you got away?"

Abbie closed her eyes. She steadied her breathing. This was the part she really didn't want to re-live. But what choice did she have? She *had* to tell her. "He had me tied to a chair. I managed to get loose. I stabbed him, then I ran."

"You stabbed him? You didn't hit him with a rock?"

"I *did* hit him with a rock. That was after he chased me through the woods."

The officer nodded and jotted down a note. "So, you remember this quite clearly? You remember stabbing him?"

Abbie could feel her patience wearing thin. "Yes. I remember grabbing the knife and sticking it into his hand. That was when I ran."

"And he chased you?"

Abbie nodded. "He knocked me down. *He* was going to stab *me*, but I managed to find a rock. I hit him with it, over and over, until my shoulder muscles ached."

"And you remember this quite clearly too?"

Abbie was frowning now - what a stupid fucking question. "Yes," she said. "Of course. Why?"

"I'm just thinking… What if…" The police officer stopped herself from finishing the sentence. She shook her head and smiled at Abbie. "Never mind."

A thought suddenly bloomed in Abbie's mind - the way this woman was speaking to her, the way she was looking at her… What if they thought *she* killed the others?

The officer stood from her chair. "Well, I think that will do for now. I'm sure you need your rest. If you think of anything else, please do let us know.

And I'll be sure to keep you informed regarding your missing friends." And then she was gone, walking out of the room with long, urgent strides, as if the whole hospital were on fire.

Abbie closed her eyes. She was exhausted. She wanted to sleep. But she couldn't sleep; she couldn't risk it. She knew that if she did sleep, her dreams would be nightmares - full of bears and monsters and death and blood.

Abbie hoped she'd never dream again.

"Knock, knock."

It was a voice Abbie recognised. Dad. Abbie opened her eyes to see her father standing in the doorway, a wide and welcoming smile on his face, both hands behind his back.

And then her mum was there too, pushing her way past Abbie's father. "Oh my God!" shrieked Abbie's mother. "My poor baby! What have they done to you?"

"Mum…" sobbed Abbie, the tears flooding her cheeks.

Her mum seemed to float across the room, skidding to her knees beside the bed, her head dropping into Abbie's lap. She took Abbie's hands in her own and squeezed. "I'm *so* sorry. My poor baby girl. We came as soon as they called."

Abbie's lungs burned as they struggled to pull in enough air, her cries becoming laboured as her tears dried up. "Mum… It was horrible. Everybody's dead! They… They killed Bex."

Abbie's mum lifted her head. She was crying too. "I know, baby. I know. But *you're* safe, that's all that matters to *me*."

"Yeah, kiddo," said Abbie's dad, strolling into the room as cool as a cucumber, as if his daughter *hadn't* just survived a traumatic, life-altering event. "You're still here. *That's* what's important."

It *wasn't* all that was important, not to Abbie. She'd lost her friends. They'd suffered horribly. Now, nothing would ever be the same again. Her life was as good as over.

But still, her parents meant no harm. They just didn't understand.

"Anyway," said Abbie's dad. "I brought you something. I hope it might make you smile."

Abbie's breath caught at the back of her throat.

Her dad pulled his hands out from behind his back, revealing to Abbie the gift he'd so kindly brought her. It was fat and brown and furry. A teddy bear. It had tiny black dots for eyes. It was wearing a glittery bow tie and a bowler hat.

Abbie stared at it. Half of her brain expected it to spring to life, to start laughing at her, to maybe even try to kill her. The other half of her brain told her this was stupid.

"Excuse me," said the police officer, poking her head back into the room. It was clear that she was speaking to Abbie's parents. "Could I speak with you both, out here in the corridor? It'll only take a second."

Abbie's mum wiped away her tears. "Of course," she said, planting a kiss on Abbie's forehead, before leaving the room.

Abbie's dad sat the teddy bear on the bed, propped up against the footboard. He too then left the room, offering Abbie a wink as he left.

It was just Abbie and the bear now. She continued to stare at it, daring it to move. Out in the hallway, she could hear her parents talking to the police officer, their voices hushed to the point where Abbie couldn't make out their words.

But it didn't matter what they were saying. Abbie really didn't care.

She was more concerned about the bear, watching her from the end of the bed, waiting for its opportunity to kill her.

Maybe she *was* crazy after all.

THE END

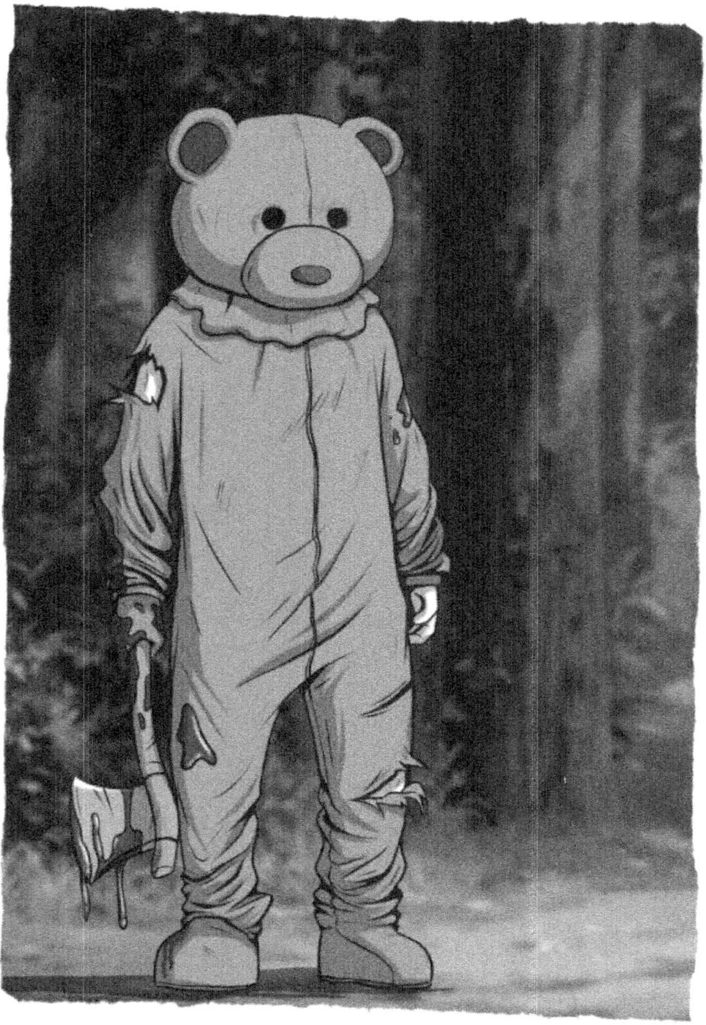

ALSO AVAILABLE

The Whores Of Satan
Bloodhounds
Superfan
Idle Hands
In The Valley Of The Cannibals
Nazi Gut Munchers
The House Of Rotting Flesh
In The Name Of The Devil
Shotgun Nun
Return To The Valley Of The Cannibals
The House Of Rotting Flesh: Episode 2
Teddy Bears Picnic
Night Of The Freaks
Shotgun Nun Vol.2: The Wrath Of God

Printed in Great Britain
by Amazon